Praise for *The Merry*

"A feast for fans of the bizarre told with such verve and originality, Jeremy C. Shipp's *The Merry Dredgers* is an experience unlike any other and proves Shipp to be a fearless and masterful storyteller."
—Eric LaRocca, author of
Things Have Gotten Worse Since We Last Spoke

"Shipp's imagination is on full display in this paranoid, claustrophobic little tale that somehow balances suspense, folk horror, and a unique brand of cult noir that is every bit as unique as its author. You'll read this in one sitting, I promise."
—Ronald Malfi, bestselling author of
Come with Me and *Black Mouth*

"Shipp paints their labyrinthine world in a stylish, snappy voice that immediately has you rooting for this underdog princess. *The Merry Dredgers* swirls a quirky outlook, strange secrets, and dark fantasy into a treat of shadow-flavored cotton candy."
—Hailey Piper, Bram Stoker Award-winning author

"A delicious Molotov cocktail of grief, paranoia, sisterhood, and bizarre dreams wrapped in a beautiful cloak of dark-as-midnight noir. *The Merry Dredgers* is unique, haunting, and weird in the best sense of the word. This is Shipp at their very best."
—Gabino Iglesias, author of
The Devil Takes You Home and *Coyote Songs*

"Immediately intriguing and written in a fun, amusing and quirky tone, *The Merry Dredgers* brings readers along for a ride not unlike those in the magical, goblin-filled kingdom Seraphina must infiltrate to seek justice for her sister. Shipp's use of the setting is second to none, making the most of the

creepy animatronics, still and fetid waters, dilapidated rides and arcades. Prepare to be entertained in the best possible ways."
—Laurel Hightower, author of *Crossroads* and *Below*

"A sharp and self-aware voice brings this wonderfully weird tale to life—full of brilliant visuals and bizarro set pieces, *The Merry Dredgers* is a work of immeasurable imagination and heart."
—Premee Mohamed, author of the Beneath the Rising trilogy

"Jeremy C. Shipp is one of contemporary horror's most original and unnerving voices. Their latest, *The Merry Dredgers*, offers up a seemingly straightforward mystery that quickly evolves into a delightfully odd and eerie tale involving a rent-a-princess, a goblin-themed amusement park, and the dark secret at the heart of a cult."
—Joseph Mallozzi, showrunner for *Stargate* and *Dark Matter*

"A story of sibling love, powerful friendship, terrible tragedy, and suspicious cultists, all delivered with Shipp's signature dreadful whimsy. Do you dare enter the mouth of the goblin? It'll change you . . ."
—Alan Baxter, award-winning author of
The Gulp and *Sallow Bend*

"Under the veneer of a weird mystery, Jeremy Shipp has written a work that explores deep questions about authenticity, identity, and relationships. You might not think a book about cults, attempted murder, and animatronic goblins could be gentle and kind, but this one? It's a warm cup of tea for the strange soul."
—Wendy N. Wagner, author of
The Secret Skin and *The Deer Kings*

"Told with the razor-sharp kaleidoscopic eye that only Shipp can deliver, *The Merry Dredgers* creates an environment

that will both perplex but also compel readers to be completely involved."
—Steve Stred, Splatterpunk-nominated author of
Sacrament, Mastodon, and *Churn the Soil*

"A unique blend of mystery, dark fantasy, and horror, Jeremy C. Shipp's *The Merry Dredgers* is equal parts amusing and thrilling. Its pages drip with whimsy and style, and with this new novel, Shipp is further carving out their own space within the horror world."
—Shane Hawk, author of *Anoka* and
co-editor of *Never Whistle at Night*

"Like Brian Evenson's *Last Days* and Will Elliott's *The Pilo Family Circus, The Merry Dredgers* immerses the reader in a world of playful dread, grim laughter, and grotesque fun. What sets Shipp's novel apart, however, is its anxious tenderness. Shipp's sharp prose forces us to engage with the pain of alienation, the yearning for connection, the risks of intimacy, and the vertigo one suffers in a world in which everyone (and everything) can't be taken at face value. What a ride!"
—Nicole Cushing, author of *Mothwoman* and *A Sick Gray Laugh*

"A kaleidoscopic nightmare assembled with the fractured pieces of a fun house mirror. A screaming merry-go-round into the psyche of a woman trying to make sense of the senseless, and finding that answers don't always bring peace. This carnival-colored mystery leads us further into the dark where animatronic goblins wage war against a Wolf King, and we discover that ghosts are just bad memories we can't let go of. Shipp's most terrifying and compassionate work by far."
—Tyler Jones, author of *Burn the Plans* and *Midas*

"Whimsical and emotional, *The Merry Dredgers* is written with Shipp's signature wit and lyrical prose. Seraphina's

journey into the heart of a mysterious cult has everything you're craving; suspense, humor, intrigue, goblins, and even a dash of romance."
—Meg Hafdahl, co-author of *The Science of Women in Horror*

"*The Merry Dredgers* is a bizarro, atmospheric fever dream given horrifying shape—a story of love for a sibling and the search for belonging wrapped in a culty mystery wrapped in a psychedelic goblin carnival with teeth. It'll chew you up and spit you out, and by the end, you won't be sure if you're laughing or screaming. Shipp knows how to entertain, and they've made sure this is one amusement park ride you'll sure as hell never forget."
—Kelsea Yu, author of *Bound Feet* and *The Bones Beneath Paris*

"Shipp skillfully skewers the cult qualities of self-actualization programs in this spooky, satirical send-up of a mind and body retreat with a shady side. . . . The details of the Dredgers' regimen of new age rituals, which appear all the more absurd for being enacted against a landscape of dilapidated rides and still functioning animatronic goblins, are consistently amusing. Readers who like their weird fiction with a dash of wry humor will eat this up."
—Publishers Weekly

"A woman's attempt to avenge her sister leads to a fantastical adventure in Jeremy C. Shipp's novel *The Merry Dredgers*. . . . a fun, offbeat mystery novel set in an unforgettable location."
—Foreword Reviews

by Jeremy C. Shipp

Vacation
Cursed
The Sun Never Rises in the Big City
The Atrocities
Bedfellow
The Merry Dredgers

Collections

In the Fishbowl We Bleed
Monstrosities
Attic Clowns
Fungus of the Heart
Sheep and Wolves

Nonfiction

Always Remember to Tip Your Ninja

the merry dredgers

jeremy c. shipp

Meerkat Press
Asheville

To everyone I've lost
who I speak with in my dreams

Table of Contents

ONE

When I first started working as a princess, I felt a little self-conscious peeking through a gap in the fence into a client's yard. Nowadays, it comes as second nature. Through a knothole, I see a French bulldog in a polka-dot bowtie, squirming on his back and sunning his round, speckled belly. I also see a rustic-looking shed with a massive window. In the window, I see the severed heads of bobcats and boars and black bears. I wonder for a moment if the hunter who owns this shed only kills animals that start with the letter *b*. No, there's a sheep's head right there. Ah, but is it a bighorn sheep?

My attention shifts away from the shed because a little girl appears with glittery stickers covering her arms like tattoo sleeves. She tickles the armpits of the French bulldog for a while, and then she lies down beside him on the well-manicured lawn. A boy with a buzzcut appears and drops a balloon onto the girl's stomach.

The taxidermy shed gives me Norman Bates vibes, but at least there are actual children at this children's party. That isn't always the case. Now and again, guys will book you for a bachelor party, or worse. I haven't experienced this myself, but I visit the princess forums and I read the stories.

Now that I'm feeling somewhat safe, I make my way to the front of the house where I make my grand entrance.

Sometimes a parent will speak with me one-on-one before leading me to the heart of the party, but most of the time I'm greeted at the door by a horde of wide-eyed, yipping children. This time around, three girls spill out of the front entrance before I can even ring the doorbell.

Children soon surround me on the front porch, and I sing the Greeting Song. Or croak is more accurate, as this is my seventh party this week and I'm losing my voice. To those children who come close enough, I gently tap them on the head with my magic wand.

After I finish singing, a young mother shakes my hand and leaves behind a smear of frosting on my glove. She tells me her name, although her voice is too soft for me to hear it, and she leads me into the house to the birthday girl, who also politely shakes my hand. While I sing the girl the Birthday Princess Song, she stares down at an astronaut doll bent in strange angles on the hardwood floor. Even when I present her with a magic wand of her very own, she takes it without looking at me and doesn't say a word. I don't mind.

I sing a couple more songs and teach the children to do the fairy tale shuffle.

Eventually, the birthday girl musters up enough courage to approach me and say, "Do you want to see my dog?"

"Oh yes," I say, in the sickly-sweet manner that feels almost normal to me at this point. "I do so love animals."

There aren't any songs in the princess guidebook that are meant for pets, but I made one up about a year ago. Through song, I tell the French bulldog that his heart is full of gold and that his nose is very cold. I won't be winning any Grammys for my lyrics, I know, but the kids gobble this ditty up.

One of the good things about princess work, compared to my other jobs, is that time almost always passes swiftly. One minute I'm painting a golden tiara onto a girl's chubby face, and the next, I'm packing my rainbow duffle bag to head out.

Before I leave the yard, the girl with stickers covering her arms hops toward me. "Are you a real princess?" she says.

"What do you think?" I say, because according to the guidebook, a princess can't answer a question about her true identity with the truth, or with a lie.

The girl stares at me with her head tilted far to the side. After a few moments of scrupulous inspection, she peels a tiger sticker off her arm and holds the object out to me. "You can have this, if you want."

"Thank you ever so much."

I take the sticker, and the girl waits silently until I press the gift onto my arm. Then she dashes away.

On my way back to the house, I have to pass by the taxidermy shed. I see a bison and bunnies and what might be a band-tailed pigeon. I see the open-mouthed face of a black bear, forever roaring in agony or anger, or some combination of the two. I wonder why the hunter only keeps the heads, and what he does with the bodies. Does he pile the headless corpses in a pickup truck and dump them gracelessly in a landfill? Does he sell the carcasses to some eccentric artist who attaches mannequin heads to the torsos and displays them in his living room?

The buzzcut kid stands near the shed with a stone in his hand that looks much too large for him to lift, but somehow he's managing the feat. He tosses the stone at the glass, and I hold my breath. Thankfully, the stone turns out to be made of foam or some other harmless material.

I keep walking.

Back inside the house, I find the young mother whispering to someone on her phone. She meets my eyes and gives me an apologetic look, and then she faces the wall and continues whispering.

"You're a talented singer," says a man standing to my side. He towers over me, wearing a *Taxi Driver* t-shirt. Throughout this afternoon, I caught this guy gaping at me on multiple occasions.

"Thank you," I say, in a voice still slightly princess-like. There are children within earshot, and I don't want to shatter the illusion.

"You have a lot of potential, and I'm not just saying that." He sits on the arm of a couch and crosses his arms over his chest. "If you've ever considered trying out for one of those singing competition shows, I could help you with that. I know people. I can help you skip all the initial auditions and fast-track you through the process. If you want to leave me your number, we can talk more about this later. What do you think?"

"That sounds great, dad twice my age with a magician's goatee. Thank you for hitting on me at a children's birthday party inside a stranger's house. There's nothing I love more." That's what I want to say, but princesses are incapable of such sarcasm.

"Thanks," I say. "But I'm not interested."

"We wouldn't have to talk about singing. People say I'm a talented conversationalist."

"I'm not interested," I say, quietly, in my own voice.

I turn around and approach the birthday girl's mother. Behind me, the goatee guy mumbles something that sounds like, "Somebody's moody."

Ultimately, waiting for the young mother to finish her phone call proves fruitless. She doesn't give me a tip. Not even a bad one. She probably doesn't know how little I'm being paid, but maybe I'm giving her too much credit.

On the drive home, my scrap heap of a sedan makes a noise like a dying pig. I don't have the cash or credit or energy to deal with a shrieking vehicle right now, so I turn up the volume of my podcast and try to drown out the cacophony. It doesn't really work.

Eventually I turn off the podcast, because I'm not paying enough attention. I'm thinking about everything I want to do tonight. There's always so much I want to do after work. But as the drive continues and the fairy tale fades, my adrenaline rush becomes an adrenaline walk, which will become an adrenaline crawl into bed. As soon as I step out of my car, I suddenly feel the full force of my exhaustion.

In my head, I can hear my friend Alvin chastising me for giving so much of myself to these silly parties. I'm wasting my talent, he says. Some casting director out there will see me for the star I am, if I just get back to the grind. Alvin's a sweet person, as far as great big liars go. How long has it been since I spoke with Alvin outside of my own head? I should call him tonight. Then again, I'm sure he's busy living a real, substantial life. He doesn't need me grumbling about my existence for thirty minutes straight.

Before heading up to my apartment, I check my mail. I pull out six postcards, each one depicting a Humpty Dumpty statue with a crack in his skull. His grin looks sadistic. The other sides of the postcards are jam-packed with microscopic scribbles that are nigh indecipherable. Even without checking for a signature, I can tell these missives are from Eff. She always did have the handwriting of a rabid mouse.

Why she sent me six postcards instead of her usual rambling phone text, I have no clue. There's a chance she'll give me some explanation in her messages, and then again, she might not. My sister can be inexplicable at times.

In my apartment, I dismantle my gown and purge my face of the ghost-white foundation and enormous purple eyelids. Transformed into a regular human being once again, I pour myself some diet soda and a splash or four of pink gin. I know it sounds weird, but try it. You'll see.

Right as I sink my aching bones into the ugliest, comfiest

couch on the planet, Heracles meows at me from across the room.

"You already have food in your dish," I say. "I can see it from here."

He meows again.

I'm a pushover, so even before taking a sip of my drink, I get up and open a small can of cat food and plop the contents onto the not-quite-as-fresh blob of food.

"Is that better?" I say.

Heracles eats, and I pet the top of his head with a fore-finger before returning to the couch.

I sip my drink and place the postcards Humpty-down on the coffee table and study the messages. Apparently, the cards come together to form one long letter, because only one missive starts with *Dear Phina*, and only one ends with *Love, Eff*.

I take another sip and squint and begin to read.

Dear Phina,

First of all, I want you to know that I'm happier now than I've ever been. Picture me grinning like a jack-o'-lantern as you read through the rest of this. Picture me with a candle inside my heart, warming me from within, never burning out. That's how I feel these days. So don't worry about me, no matter what pessimistic ideas come to your mind in the next few minutes.

Anyway, I'm writing to you primarily because I want to catch up, but I also need a little help. I should probably start by telling you that a few months ago I joined a really cool community. I know when I say the word community, you're automatically going to think the word cult. I know you can't help yourself. I also know that when I assure you I'm not in a cult, you're going to think, "That's exactly what someone in a cult would say." But really, Phina, this place is more of a mind and body retreat than anything else. We're all about self-actualization and meditation and shit like that. I can already imagine the multipage rant you're planning on sending me about why I'm definitely in a cult and I'm being brainwashed, so let me help ease—

The first postcard ends abruptly at this point. Since Eff didn't take the time to indicate the order of the cards, I have to search through them all and guess which one comes next. Ah, this one seems right.

—some of your concerns before you scream them at me. One: no one here has asked me for money. Not the owner of the retreat, not the followers. Nobody. Honestly, these are the least greedy people I've ever come across. Two: I'm not being exploited, in any sense of the word. The leader of the retreat isn't some sex-crazed maniac who wants me as his fourteenth wife. Three: no one is keeping me from returning to the big wide world, and I can do so whenever I feel like it. You might think it's strange that I'm writing to you on postcards instead of texting, but none of us use phones or computers here. Before you ask: no one forced me to get rid of my phone. I wanted to break my addiction, for my own sake. We do have an emergency landline, so it's not like we can't call a plumber if the pipes burst. We're not super isolated. I also thought writing you letters would be fun. Isn't this fun? Three: wait, I already wrote three. Damn it. Now I can't remember what other points I wanted to make here, but maybe I'll think of them later. Even after all my reassurances, I'm sure you're still worried as hell about me, and I guess I appreciate that. You're a good sister. Hopefully I've at least—

The postcard ends here.

I find the next one.

—alleviated your fears a fraction of an inch. Anyway, like I mentioned earlier, I do have a small favor to ask of you. I'm sure your anxiety is through the roof right now, so remember to picture me with my jack-o'-lantern face and my cinnamon candle heart. I'm fine. I'm better than fine. Recently though I told a few of my friends here about George the Demon. I told them about what George did to me. For the most part, everyone here reacted very supportively. These are nice people, Phina. There is one guy, though, who keeps joking about how he wants to find George and break his legs or throw him down a well or stuff like that. I'm ninety-five percent sure that he's joking, but then again, guys who joke like this aren't always joking. The joking in itself didn't worry me too much until I started having some disturbing visions about George. I know you're the Scully to my Mulder, and you don't believe in psychic powers or visions or shit. I don't know if you're capable of doing so, but I want—

I grab the next postcard.

—you to attempt to turn off your preconceived notions about reality for a second and open your mind to the possibility that psychic phenomena are a natural part of our world. Did you do it? You probably didn't. Whether you believe me or not, I've always been a little bit psychic. I don't know if you remember, but Auntie Gloria thought you and me both had links to otherworldly forces, and she knew what she was talking about. She could tell when the phone was about to ring and when someone was coming to the door. You can't deny that we both dreamed about losing dad before anyone even knew he was sick. I've never taken my powers too seriously until I started living at the retreat. We cultivate

an atmosphere of self-discovery here. We spend time alone, meditating, gazing into our own souls. It's difficult to explain with words. Honestly, I've always been a little afraid of that part of myself that sees beyond normal perceptions. Here, though, that part of me feels like it's waking up. And I like it, most of the time. I'm learning to control it. I'm learning that this mystical aspect of myself is as normal as my jack-o'-lantern smile or my candle heart. I know you don't believe any of this but I—

I fumble for the next postcard.

—hope you can be happy for me, nevertheless. I'm finally starting to feel like the real Eff. It's scary. And exhilarating. I sit in a dark room, alone, and I'm inundated with the citrusy scent of peonies and the crackling of a campfire and the feeling of sticking your hand in a barrel of dried beans and so much beautiful shit like that. This is how I experience my gift most of the time. Every once in a while though, I see George with shards of glass in his face and part of his bone sticking out of his arm. I feel his terror like it's my own. My main problem is that I don't know what these images and feelings mean. Am I seeing something that's already happened, or will happen, or might? What I'm afraid of is that my friend who keeps joking about hurting George actually went through with it. He left the community for a few days recently, and I can't stop thinking about it. I'm probably worrying over nothing. Nevertheless, I was wondering if you could check on the Demon for me? Make sure he's—

Here's the next one.

—alive and breathing? He was always such a damn luddite, so you might have to go check up on him in person. I'm

eighty percent sure that these visions are nothing to worry about. Maybe George is going to die forty years from now, and that's what I'm experiencing. Maybe part of me needs to experience his passing so that he can stop living like some almighty demigod inside my head. He's a pathetic mortal, just like the rest of us. That's one theory anyway. Whatever the case may be, it would do me a world of good if you could see how George is doing. I would be forever in your debt, although I suppose I already am. Anyway, how have you been? Are you still a princess?

Love, Eff

For I-don't-know-how-many seconds, I stare at Eff's signature, as if I can scry some secret meaning from the way she signed her name. I can't.

I stack the postcards in order and place them in the drawer of the coffee table, where I keep all the important bills and papers I need to deal with posthaste. Leaning back on the couch again, I notice Heracles curled up on the threadbare cushion beside me. He rolls onto his back and when I pet his belly, he gently grabs hold of me with his claws and gnaws on my hand.

"Let go, Hare," I say.

What I need to do, first and foremost, is to think carefully about everything Eff told me. I wish I could do this now, but I'm the sort of tired that even caffeine can't fix. My sister wants me to picture her as some jubilant pumpkin. Well, picture me as a popped party balloon. Picture me as a stone made of foam, incapable of smashing a single window. That's the sort of tired I am.

I get into bed, because the sooner I sleep, the sooner I can figure out where to go from here. Right now, all I know for sure is that my sister definitely joined a cult, and I need to find a way to save her.

TWO

The next morning is a hectic phantasmagoria of screams and brightly colored vomit and two dozen children dressed as ghosts. When I first get to the party, I ask the parents if they want me to act like a princess or the ghost of a princess, and the dad says earnestly, "What's the difference?" And I don't have a good answer to that question. Toward the end of the party, the birthday boy asks me how I died. The princess guidebook doesn't specify how to answer such a question, so I tell him I died of old age.

"Are you sure you weren't eaten by a dragon?" he says.

"Oh, that's right," I say. "It was a dragon. I forgot."

In all the chaos of the morning, I don't have much time to think about Eff and her letter. When I do think about my sister, I mostly imagine her wearing sunset-colored robes or an all-black tracksuit with black-and-white sneakers. I imagine her sitting cross-legged in a damp, dark basement, wearing a pink velvet dress with puffed sleeves, with images of George's broken body whorling above her head.

Between my first party of the day and my second, I have a few minutes to sit in my car and use my phone to investigate the return address Eff included on one of the postcards. The Post Office box is located about three hours northwest of here in the meager city of Lonbloom. As far as I can tell, there aren't any cults located in the city itself. There is a fundamentalist Christian community two hours from Lonbloom, but there's no way Eff would go for that after everything our mother put us through. Also, didn't Eff mention meditation in her letter? Wouldn't Christian cultists find the whole concept of meditation to be diabolical? Just in case I'm wrong about all this, I write down the name of the cult in my note app.

The alarm clock on my phone meows at me, so I touch up my makeup using the rearview mirror, and then I ascend an impossibly steep flight of steps to party number two.

I woke up this morning calm and collected and only a little sick to my stomach. Now though, my anxiety is a tangled ball of barbed wire writhing in my torso. During those rare moments when no one's paying any attention to me, I stare at a blooming jacaranda tree in the client's yard. I think about the girl with sticker arms whispering into the French bulldog's ear and then using a finger to draw a cross over his ribs. I think about this morning, when I placed my long satin gloves on the couch and Heracles grabbed one in his mouth and dashed away. These thoughts do calm me down, slightly.

Toward the end of the party, I'm painting scales and fangs onto a pigtailed girl's face, and a memory, or a set of memories really, floats to the surface of my consciousness. I remember standing outside the library with Eff, looking at the raptorial grotesque carved into one of the pillars. The carving glared at us with his mouth agape, and we slowly slid our hands inside. Eff liked to tell me that one day when we least expected it the mouth would bite down. I hated the game, really, but I never refused to play.

"Do I look scary?" the little girl says, after I'm done painting her face.

"Oh yes," I say. "You are wonderfully terrifying indeed."

Satisfied, the girl walks away and hisses at no one in particular.

After the party, the father of the birthday girl smiles conspiratorially while handing me a folded-up ten-dollar tip. He tells me to look out for my wicked stepmother. Since he says this in a goofy, non-creepy way, I tell him, "I always do."

Back in my rust bucket, I pick up a veggie burger and some fried mushrooms from a drive-through and eat in the parking lot. I only have one more party scheduled for today, so I check what jobs are available in the meantime on my pet sitting app. While I'm accepting assignments, an enormous glob of ketchup dives onto my dress. But it doesn't really matter. When you're around children as often as I am, getting your gown dirty is an inevitability. It's your destiny. I attack the stain with a gossamer-thin napkin and then put the matter out of my mind.

By force of habit, I unpause the podcast on my phone. However, I quickly realize that I'm in no mood to hear about a serial killer who utilizes his victims' hair and eyelashes when creating ball-jointed porcelain dolls.

In silence, I probe deeper into the fundamentalist Christian cult, and I imagine Eff wearing a pastel prairie dress that reaches down to her ankles. According to the website I'm looking at, the women are required to pray for two hours every morning while sitting under a fig tree. The men beat their children with sticks if they misbehave. There's no mention of meditation or psychic powers or self-actualization. I'm definitely meandering in the wrong direction, so where do I go from here?

I sigh and turn away from my phone. Outside my window, a man sitting on a circular tree bench raises one finger and the pit-bull–lab beside him barks. When the man raises two fingers, the dog barks twice. The guy notices me looking, stands up and walks the couple steps over to my car. I roll down my window.

"Do you have a spare coin or two?" he says.

I give him two dollars, and the man pretends to tip a hat at me. He's not actually wearing one.

"I like your dog," I say.

"Say thank you to the nice woman," the man says.

The dog barks, once, and then the two of them return to their bench. After the man holds up three fingers, the dog barks four times. Close. To be honest, I could keep watching this all day, but I have things to do. Snakes to feed. A sister to save.

I give the man a little wave, and he returns my gesture with a deep bow. Maybe because I'm still dressed like a cartoon princess, but who knows, really?

The drive to the first pet owner's house is more than a little stressful, thanks to the worries flurrying in my mind, as well as a near-collision with a swerving Tacoma. On the drive, I decide that for my next course of action, I should write Eff a letter. I need to convince the most stubborn person this side of the Mississippi to somehow abandon her new grinning-like-a-jack-o'-lantern life.

In my client's attic, I dangle a wriggling mouse by the tail and transport him from a cheerless, stark cage to a luxurious vivarium packed with cork bark tubes and grapewood branches and bushy fern plants.

Soon, Mrs. Checkers the kingsnake glides out of her hiding spot. She whips at the air with a forked, burgundy-colored tongue.

These days, most snake owners feed their pets thawed or freshly killed rodents. But according to the note on my phone, Mrs. Checkers refuses to eat anything that she doesn't kill herself. The note also says that the problem with live mice is that sometimes they fight back. So if I see the mouse biting or clawing at the snake, I'm supposed to intervene. Intervene how exactly, I have no idea. The note doesn't specify.

Thankfully, Mrs. Checkers incapacitates the mouse with

her first strike and then strangles him without any complications. The mouse's tail stops twitching.

"I'm sorry," I say.

I imagine a Lilliputian version of Eff sitting cross-legged in the vivarium, her eyes closed in meditation.

While feeding the other reptiles and amphibians in the attic, I painstakingly compose half a dozen letters to Eff in my mind. Each one is less impressive than the last. I try to scare her. I try to touch her heart. I try to appeal to her more rational angels. As I'm dumping frozen cubes of bloodworms into an axolotl tank, a thought crosses my mind. The thought is so ludicrous that I snort out loud. I can't be serious.

But before I know it, I'm parking near the Demon's colonial-style house, under a purple orchid tree. The shadow of the plant doesn't hide my car, but I feel irrationally safer nonetheless. I put on my colossal aviator sunglasses and slouch down in my seat as far as possible. As I search the myriad windows for any signs of life, I realize that I'm holding my breath. I need to calm down. Even if the Demon spots me, he probably won't recognize me, what with my sunglasses and my princess makeup and my bone-white wig. Right? A droplet of cold sweat runs down my back.

For fifteen minutes or so, I surveil the house in complete silence, but then I get bored. I put in my earbuds. I'm still not in the mood to hear about a serial killer who filled his porcelain dolls with dehydrated chicken gizzards, so I switch to a Flaming Lips playlist.

If only George didn't hate computers, I could stalk him online like a normal person, and find out everything I need to know. As it is, I'm stuck here staring pointlessly at an empty house. Maybe I should search the mailbox. At the very least, I could verify that George still lives here. Maybe I should talk to the neighbors. These are intriguing ideas indeed, but I'm too much of a coward to exit the car.

All of a sudden, the Demon barrels toward my driver's side window. At least, that's what I think I'm seeing for a split second. Instead, a middle-aged woman in a Gucci tracksuit jogs by my car, pushing a grinning Pomeranian in one of those three-wheeled exercise strollers.

"Calm down," I say.

I'm not sure how long a reasonable person would sit here twiddling her thumbs, waiting for something to happen, but I likely passed that threshold a while back now. I'm a couple more negative thoughts away from giving up on this whole operation when a BMW convertible rolls slowly into the driveway.

George steps out of the passenger seat, with casts on his left arm and his right leg. A deep-looking cut stretches from the bridge of his nose to below his ear. I can't believe what I'm seeing. I can't believe my luck.

A young woman with doe eyes like Eff hands George a crutch, and then he turns and looks directly at my car. I almost duck down in my seat, but I don't want to call any extra attention to myself, do I? After a second, George turns away from me and points at the back of his convertible. The young woman quickly pops the trunk.

I'm still so shocked by the sight of George that for a while I don't move a muscle. Thankfully, I remember my mission and manage to snap a quick photo of George before he and his girlfriend enter the house.

I can't get over the fact that Eff was right. I'm sure her psychic visions are nonsense, but maybe that cultist friend of hers actually attacked George. I was almost positive that Eff was wrong about her suspicions, but I'm glad I checked. Now when I write Eff a letter, I can include this photo. Maybe the image of George's sliced up face will be enough to scare her away from her new friends.

"I should find out more," I say out loud, my voice cracking.

But I don't move, because a face-to-face conversation with the Demon is the last thing in the world I want to do. Maybe there's something else I can try.

As soon as I step out of my car, I feel like I need to throw up. My anxiety's now an open-mouthed face of a black bear, forever roaring in fear.

I take a deep breath. What I need is to think of all this as a performance. I need to picture myself as a noir detective, dressed in a tan overcoat and a wide-brim fedora worn at an angle.

I glance over at George's house. I see two silhouettes in the living room where the curtains are drawn. They won't see me. I repeat the sentence over and over to myself, to make it true. They won't see me. They won't see me.

I walk away from the safety of my car and the purple orchid tree.

Swiftly and clumsily, I make my way down the cobble-stone path next door to George, lined with garden gnomes and stone hedgehogs. On the front porch, a dozen metal frogs sit at the edge of the deck, dangling fishing lines over the side.

When I knock, an elderly woman answers the front door. She gives me one of those looks that says she didn't expect a woman in a full-length satin gown with long white gloves to materialize at her door.

"Can I help you?" the woman says.

"Hi," I say. "I'm a singing telegram. I'm here for George Davenport." I don't know if singing telegrams still exist any-where in the world, but this is the best I can come up with on the fly.

Signs of relief transform the woman's face. "Oh, George is our neighbor. You're going to want the tall house right over there."

"Oops," I say. "Sorry to bother you."

The woman waves off the thought. "It's no bother at all."

"I . . . the woman who hired me told me about what happened to George," I say, trying to saturate my tone with congeniality. "It's a shame." Why a singing telegram would be privy to such information, I have no idea. I'm doing my best here.

"Yes," the woman says. "Poor George. How someone could do that to another person, I'll never know."

"Yeah," I say. I need to probe her for more information, but I'm not sure what to say next. I'm panicking, so all I manage is to thank her and say goodbye.

On my way to the next house over, I push away the freaked out, bungling Seraphina. That's not me anymore. Picture me with gum rubber shoes and a 38 Smith and Wesson Special in a leather shoulder holster. My only weakness is femme fatales with legs for days and wide, crooked smiles.

After I press the doorbell, a young woman answers wearing black yoga pants and an oversized tank top. A child screams a song about tuna somewhere behind her.

"Hi," I say. "I'm sorry to bother you. I'm a friend of George Davenport, your neighbor."

A look of fear, and possibly pity, transforms her face for a moment. There's a chance that she's caught a glimpse of the Demon behind George's mask.

"No, I'm lying," I say. "I'm not his friend. I know what kind of person he is. He used to date my sister, and it's important that I find out some information about him. I could explain to you why I need this information, but it's a whole big thing, and you don't have time for a long story, I'm guessing. Is there any way you could help me with this? I just have a few questions."

The young woman stares at the ketchup stain on my dress. As soon as she notices me noticing her, she turns her attention to my face.

"Okay," she says, not unkindly. "What do you want to know?"

"Do you know what happened to him? George?"

The woman glances over in the direction of the Demon's house. "It was a hit-and-run. It happened about a week and a half ago. I'm not sure where."

"Did they catch the person who did it?"

"No. I don't think so."

From somewhere inside the house, the child says, "Mom! I'm turning into a frog!"

I can feel myself panicking again. My time's running out here, and I'm not sure what else to ask.

"I . . . did you hear anything about the car? The one that hit him?"

"George was hit from behind," the woman says, casually, as if she's commenting on the weather. "According to his girlfriend, he didn't see anything. She's the one who told me all this."

The child now materializes at his mother's side, wearing a cracked, plastic frog mask.

"Are you a princess?" the child says.

"Sometimes," I say.

"I'd better go," the mother says. "Good luck with helping your sister."

"Thank you," I say. This is the longest conversation I've had with someone using my real voice in who-knows-how long, and I feel the pathetic urge to keep talking. Part of me wants to sit at this stranger's cluttered dining table and drink Diet Coke or boxed apple juice or whatever she has on hand and tell her everything I know about Eff and the cult.

As I'm heading back to my car, I hear a door opening in the direction of the Demon's house. I tell myself that I'm probably being paranoid, but when I turn my head, I see the young woman with doe eyes moving hurriedly in my direction. Then

I notice George standing in the doorway with a tiny grin on his face. I guess he does recognize me, and he's commanded his girlfriend to do what exactly?

I speed-walk to my car, stumbling once on nothing in particular. I manage to defy the laws of physics and not fall on my face. As I fumble with my keys, the woman says, "Excuse me." She sounds close. She sounds like she could reach out and touch my back if she wanted to.

"I'm sorry," I say. "I have an appointment and I'm in a rush."

Only after I'm in my car with the door locked do I glance over at the girl. She's standing a few feet away, with her arms crossed over her four-hundred-dollar blouse. She gives me an exasperated look, which hurts my feelings more than it should.

I drive away, slowly, as if I don't have a care in the world. I don't look back at George, but his small venomous smile invades my thoughts regardless. That poor girl. I pray for her, despite the fact that I don't believe in God. I pray that the doe-eyed girl is friends with the young mother two houses down. I pray that someday soon she'll escape the nightmarish maze she doesn't even know she's trapped within.

As I head to my next job, I compose another letter in my head. This one feels right on the money. I tell Eff about the hit-and-run, and how her cult friend could be responsible, for all we know. I tell her that she means the world and a bean to me, which is something our father used to say. I didn't think to ask him what "world and a bean" means exactly until after he was gone. I asked Aunt Gloria what it meant once, but she didn't know. In my imagination, Eff sits cross-legged in a damp, dark basement, reading my letter. Once she finishes, she snickers a little through her nose and says, "Oh Phina." Even in my imagination, I can't change her mind.

Then I picture a black-and-white version of myself sitting at a massive desk in front of venetian blinds and a sign etched into the glass of the door that says *Seraphina Ramon*: *Princess Detective Agency*. I've never lost a case. What do I have to worry about? I'll convince Eff somehow. Suddenly, the whole exercise feels a bit too silly, and my noir persona drains out of me, through the floor of my car, into a pothole. My confidence plummets downward, toward the center of the earth.

The one thing keeping me from pulling over and ugly-crying uncontrollably is that Eff is tough as hell. When she found herself trapped in George's brambly maze, she trudged her way through the twists and turns, all the way to the exit. After our father died, I would come home from school and lie in bed, imagining my room like a giant coffin. I pretended that giant earthworms wriggled in circles around my walls. Sometimes Eff ventured into my grave and asked me to play, and I pinched her arm. And when she left my room, I pinched myself. Eff didn't give up though, and eventually, after who-knows-how-many-weeks, I started playing again. Eff dragged me to the tiny park by our apartment complex after school. In her spaceship, she flew me to worlds populated by talking hedgehogs and affable pirates. We blew up evil planets made of metal and bones. We rescued cosmic orphans from the clutches of the Nothing Man, who ate shadows for breakfast and who, with a touch, could make you lose your sense of taste or smell. We built these worlds together. Eff called me captain, even though she made most of the decisions. Thanks to these adventures, sometimes I didn't think about our father's death for hours at a time. When we were teenagers, Eff was the only one who stood up to our mother. Even after a slap to the face or a remote thrown at her head, Eff wouldn't back down. She was the first one to say goodbye to our mother forever, when Eff was old enough to survive on her own.

The point is, if someone can escape some bizarre cult, it's Eff. She's going to be fine. I repeat the thought over and over and over, and eventually I almost believe it.

THREE

Everything happens so fast. One minute I'm battling a giant inflatable dragon with my foam magic wand, and the next the world is crumbling apart. In general, I don't answer my phone while I'm working, but I don't want to miss a call from Eff. The cult might have destroyed her phone, so who knows what number she'll call me from. So I answer, and a woman with a nasally voice gives me some story about Eff falling into a quarry. She calls it an accident. She gives me the name of the hospital. I want to believe this is some sort of prank. Maybe the cultists want me to believe Eff is hurt for some reason. If Eff's unconscious, how would the hospital even get my name and number? Then I remember. After Eff ODed years ago, I printed out an emergency contact card for her to keep in her bag.

I still don't fully trust the woman on the phone. She's one of the cultists for all I know. So once I escape the birthday party into my car, I call the Lonbloom Police Department and I end up speaking to a detective who gives me the same rubbish story as the woman on the phone. I only have time to ask a few questions before the detective excuses himself and hangs up. At least I get the name of the quote-unquote retreat where the so-called accident happened.

I head home, and with each passing moment, I become more panicked. This is feeling real. In my apartment, I dump out the magical contents of my duffle bag and with my hands trembling, I pack up Eff's postcards and some clothes and my makeup box. I empty three cans of cat food on top of each other into the bowl, and I kiss Heracles on the top of his head. Before I leave, I call the police department again and make an appointment.

Three hours later, I'm at Lonbloom Hospital in a room congested with tangles of tubes and wires, and my little sister in the center of it all. She looks like our dad did in his final days. I try not to think about him. I can't handle his hospital room pushing its way into my head while I'm trying to cope with this one.

When the doctor speaks to me, she sounds a little like the adults in a Peanuts cartoon. "Wa wa wa wa wa structural injuries wa wa wa wa wa neurological impairment wa wa wa wa brainstem function wa wa." She goes on like this for a while, and when she's done, I ask her if she can please say that again. She asks me which part she wants me to repeat. I say everything.

This time around, I understand her more clearly. Or at least, I hear what she's saying. She says that comas are never a walk in the park, but that Eff's CT scan doesn't show any major structural injuries. Eff's brainstem is also showing some function. Her pupils respond to light, for example. She can even initiate breaths on her own. The doctor says that we can't know for sure the severity of her brain injuries, because the scans don't reveal everything. Within a month, we'll know more. Comas rarely last longer than a month. She says that even in the best possible scenario, Eff won't wake up fully conscious and fully herself. There are various stages of recovery, and she might move through them quickly, and she might not. In the worst-case scenario, she won't move through them at all. She tells me not to give up hope. She tells me that she'll do everything she can.

"Okay," I say quietly, and I glance over at Eff, and I can feel warm tears stinging the corners of my eyes. I should have saved her when I had the chance. I thought I would have more time, but they did this to her before I could make any real headway beyond mailing my stupid letter to the Post Office box.

The doctor tells me something else, but I can't hear her again. I'm focused on the rhythmic wheezing of the ventilator. Why does she need a ventilator if she can initiate her own breaths? I could ask the doctor, but I decide to look it up online later when I can think.

"Try to keep that in mind," the doctor says.

"I will," I lie, as I have no idea what she's referring to.

"Do you have any other questions for me?"

"Not right now." The words sound brusque coming out of my mouth. I don't mean them to be. I want to apologize, and tell her that I appreciate everything she's doing, but there's no time. The doctor gives me a sympathetic smile and leaves me with my sister.

For some reason, I didn't expect to be left alone here in an ICU room. The atmosphere feels too treacherous. What if I accidentally bump into some vital piece of machinery? What if I hold Eff's hand, ignorant of the fact that this is against the rules? They made me wash my hands before I came in here, but does that mean I can touch her? What else should I know? I take a deep breath.

I approach Eff's bedside, and I stare at her sallow, mangled face. What disturbs me the most isn't so much the tubes and cuts and bruises, but how calm she looks while enduring all these torments.

It's such a waste for Eff to be here in this bed, so silent

and still. She might be a fuck-up of epic proportions, but at least she takes every opportunity to enjoy her life. She literally says things like "every day is a gift" and she means it. She lives it. I've seen her build massive sculptures of goddesses out of chicken wire and trash. I've seen her have fun at the DMV. Eff's a bright, wandering light in a fucked-up world, and she shouldn't be here. If I could throw myself off a cliff and shatter my skull and take her place here, I would.

"Hi," I say, and I carefully wipe the tears from my eyes. "It's me."

I should have asked the doctor if there's a chance that Eff can hear me. I'm clueless here. Beyond what the doctor told me just now, everything I know about comas I learned from half-watching General Hospital with Aunt Gloria when I was ten.

I clear my throat and say, "I don't know if you read my letter. If you did, I probably hurt your feelings, and I'm sorry about that. I was being overly patronizing. I know you hate when I get like that. Everything I told you was important, but I didn't have to be a condescending garbage person." I squeeze three fingers of my left hand with my right. I squeeze them so hard they hurt. I should stop being such a downer, because maybe she can hear me after all. What Eff needs right now is positivity. Right? If we were having a normal conversation on a normal day, Eff would be asking to hear one of my semi-bullshit stories about my life. She loves my bullshit.

I clear my throat again and say, "I should tell you about this thing that happened to me a couple months ago. Through the princess app, I was contacted by a woman who said her daughter was drawing all over their house. She drew on the walls, the floor, the lightbulbs, the contents of her dad's wallet. When the parents hid away all the markers and pens and crayons, the girl started drawing with ketchup and with shampoo and so on. According to the girl, her imaginary friend Princess Pancake told her to do it. Her parents tried to reason with the girl, and they even tried reasoning with Pancake, but nothing worked. Eventually, the mother tried dressing up as Pancake in order to convince the girl to stop. But the girl could easily see through the disguise. That's when they turned to me. They thought a professional might help." I realize that I'm still squeezing the same three fingers, so I release them. "Of course, I'm not supposed to go to a client's house when a birthday party isn't taking place. But I was late on rent and the mother promised me a mind-boggling tip. So I went. Their home was a beige nightmare of a McMansion with nothing but a sea of asphalt out front. Inside, the mother led me into a walk-in closet. She chooses this moment to reveal to me that yes, Pancake is a princess, but she has the head of a bird. So she opens this old Versace box and pulls out a high-end parrot mask with a beak that opens and closes mechanically when you speak."

At this point, Eff would say something like, "That is some wild shit."

Normally, she would be studying my face carefully as I speak, trying to discern which parts of my story are true, and which parts are lies. Of course, Eff was the one who came up with this game. She's good at it. She can read me, and not because of some psychic sisterly bond like Aunt Gloria liked to believe. Eff's good at this game because she knows me. I continue, "And I know what you're thinking, but all of this is true so far. The mother handed me the mask and told me she'd add two hundred dollars to the tip if I went through with the job. So I did. I put on the mask and the mother led me to the five-year-old. In my best princess voice, I told her I was the real Pancake and that I only wanted her to draw on pieces of paper from now on. As soon as I said that, the girl burst into tears, and the mother told me to—"

Suddenly, an alarm goes off that pierces me to the center

of my bones. The sound's coming from one of Eff's machines. I expect someone to rush in straightaway, but no one comes. I hurry outside and spot a stern-looking nurse.

"We need help!" I say.

The woman saunters over to me, as if she has all the time in the world.

"We need help," I say again.

"I'm sure everything's fine," the woman says, following me into the room.

While the nurse tinkers with one of the machines, I keep my eyes on Eff. I watch her chest rising and falling.

After a moment, the clamoring of the machine ceases, and my bones stop aching.

"She's fine," the nurse says, gently. "Alerts go off all the time here, sweetie. I know they sound urgent, but most of the time they're not. Honestly, most of what you'll hear are false alarms. Someone should have explained that to you when you first came in."

"Okay," I say. "So she's okay?"

"Yes. We'll take good care of her."

The nurse leaves, and I realize then that I should have thanked her for being so kind.

I'm too rattled to finish my story, so instead, I sit silently in the high-back chair in the corner of the room. After a few seconds, I drag the chair over to Eff's bedside. I still need to ask someone if it's safe to hold her hand.

Time passes, and sometimes I feel numb, and sometimes I feel everything. Sometimes I hear the ventilator. Sometimes I hear my father gasping for breath. Every time a nurse comes in, I half-expect them to kick me out, because visiting hours ended a while back. But they never do. I never do finish my bullshit story about Pancake and the little girl. I wonder how it would have ended. I wonder if Eff would have guessed that I made up the part about the bird head because of the planet of bird-headed people we liked to visit on our space adventures in the park.

Eventually, I feel too exhausted and too hungry to sit here anymore. As soon as I exit the hospital, a whirlpool of guilt churns inside me. How can I leave her at a time like this? What if she regains consciousness and the first thing she sees is an empty chair beside her? The worst part is the relief I feel getting out of there, away from the wires and tubes and Eff's frail body and the phantom of my father dying again everywhere I looked. I know I shouldn't think about myself at a time like this, but I'm weak. I don't know how to get through this.

For a while, I sit in my car in the hospital parking lot, trying to take deep breaths and eating cold, ancient fries. Part of me wants to drive the three hours back to my apartment tonight, even though I'll have to drive right back in the morning. I want to sleep in my own bed with a softly snoring Heracles curled up behind my head on his bee-print pillow. I want my home.

But I quickly give up on the idea, because I'm the sort of tired that all the caffeine in the universe can't fix. I end up at a knockoff Motel 6 that I'd rate as a Motel 1.5, if I'm being generous. The room works hard to antagonize me, what with the '70s-style wood paneling and the vomit-colored carpet. The air smells like Clorox and dead skunk, and as for the bed, I feel as if I'm lying on some rough-edged wooden sculpture.

Maybe I'm being a bit unfair here. Maybe I'm just devastated beyond repair and this room is the nearest punching bag.

Thankfully, I only spend a few minutes tossing and turning in this hellhole before falling asleep. Next thing I know, I'm wandering around a dimly lit farmhouse, dressed in a heavy, gray nightgown that's much too long for me. I keep stepping on the hem. Despite having lived in this house for who-knows-how-many years, I can't remember exactly how to get to the living room. What's wrong with me? Eventually, I manage to stumble my way to my destination. I approach the wood-burning stove nestled in an alcove made of gnarled, pallid bricks. I should add another piece of firewood to the burnt-orange embers, but there aren't any logs left on the storage rack. All that remains on the rack is a stiff, dead raccoon lying on his back, his mouth wide open, his eyes liquefied and dripping from their sockets. My stomach churns with disgust inside me. Someone left him here so that I could burn him on the fire, but I refuse. I need to chop more wood. As I head for the back door, I notice Heracles and his three sisters clinging motionlessly to the screen door. Maybe they want to go outside. I pet Heracles, and I'm disturbed by how ossified his fur feels. I should take him to the vet tomorrow, first thing. The moment I swing open the screen door, someone or something saturates the house with a metallic cacophony. I release the door and head into the kitchen.

Someone's standing next to my walnut table, facing the wall. He's dressed in a black t-shirt and slim-fit jeans. An overpowering moldy scent attacks my nose, but I can't see anything rotting anywhere in the room.

"Excuse me," I say.

He doesn't respond in any way, so I move closer. The redwood floor creaks with each step.

"Excuse me," I say again. "Is that you, George?" I try to look at the man's face, but he turns away from me. The back of his head appears perfectly combed. There's not a single hair out of place.

"You need to go," I say.

I try again and again to get a better look, but no matter where I position myself in the kitchen, he faces away from me. Every so often, I catch a glimpse of an open book cradled in his hands. When I try to focus on the text, the words swarm around the pages like hundreds of angry flies.

"Please go," I say.

What starts out as a low-pitched wheezing intensifies into a booming growl. The man's neck trembles and he drops the book on the floor. His fingers twitch at his sides. Soon, his whole body vibrates. I cover my ears with my hands. He turns to face me, but I don't want to see any more of him. I run in the opposite direction. As soon as I can see the back door, the cats drop off the screen and hit the floor with loud clunks. They rest silently with their legs straight up in the air, their faces misshapen, their eyes bloated and ready to pop.

That's the last thing I see before opening my eyes in the Motel 2.5. I'm giving the place an extra point because I didn't wake up once during the night. No one banged on my door or screamed through the wall, and that has to count for something.

Still half-asleep, I shuffle into the bathroom and begin slathering my face with the pastiest of foundation. Then I freeze. This is the first step in my princess makeup routine. I stare at myself in the mirror and warp my mouth into an exaggerated frown, for no particular reason.

After washing off the princess paste, I begin again, and I transform myself into the most professional version of myself I can manage. I use a foundation that actually matches my skin tone. The lipstick I pick transforms my muted pink lips into slightly shiny muted pink lips. I wear the black pencil skirt Aunt Gloria bought me years ago that I wear to every job interview and funeral. There's a monstrous, mysterious green stain on the blouse I wanted to wear, but thankfully I also packed a sky blue button-down that should do the trick. Once I'm done dressing, I stand in front of the mirror. I don't know if I look like someone a detective would take seriously, but this is the best I can do.

An hour or so later, I'm at the police station, and a woman leads me to a smallish cubicle with a cluster of vintage postcards push-pinned to the wall. On a shelf to the left of the computer, there's a lint roller standing straight up and a mug that reads *World's Greatest Magician*. All of this surprises me, somewhat. I guess part of me expected to speak with the detective in one of those interrogation rooms with uncomfortable metal chairs and a black pendant light dangling above my head.

The woman who led me here waves her hand at a rolling office chair that tilts slightly to the side. "You can wait here," she says.

I take a seat, and I spend a few minutes studying the vintage postcards. Most of them are illustrations of state capital buildings from around the country. There's also one featuring a magician in a black suit sitting on a throne with a tiny red devil on his shoulder whispering in his ear. A woman in a white flapper dress levitates above his head. What is it with this guy and magicians? Does he do magic tricks in his spare time? Maybe this is some in-joke between him and his colleagues?

After a million years or so, Detective Burns finally shows up and shakes my hand with a damp palm. He's wearing a grotesque black-and-yellow striped tie that I can't keep my eyes off of.

"Good morning, Ms. Ramon," he says. "Firstly, I'm so sorry about what happened to your sister. I'll be praying for her quick recovery."

"Thank you," I say.

"Secondly, I appreciate you arranging to speak with me today. Your sister's lucky to have someone like you looking out for her." He glances at the file folder on my lap. "On the phone, you said you have something you want to show us?"

"Yeah," I say, and I open the file folder. This morning, I debated with myself about whether or not I should show him the postcards. What with all of Eff's talk about psychic visions, I'm afraid the detective might dismiss everything she wrote as nonsense. But ultimately, I need him to know that I'm basing my suspicions on more than my own gut instinct.

So I show him the copies I made of the postcards at the Lonbloom Public Library with certain passages highlighted in yellow. I show him the photo of George with the marked-up casts on his left arm and his right leg. I tell him that according to a neighbor, the hit-and-run occurred a week and a half before I received the postcards, and so it's plausible that the cultist was the one responsible. And if this is the sort of people that we're dealing with, it's possible that my sister's accident wasn't an accident at all.

The detective listens to all this attentively enough. When I'm finished, he says, "Well. That's certainly an interesting theory, Ms. Ramon. As we mentioned on the phone earlier, all the evidence we've gathered so far suggests that what happened to your sister is an accident. The toxicology report verifies that your sister was drinking excessively that night, and according to the other guests at the retreat, she would often take walks alone in the dark. There's evidence that the ground crumbled under her feet when she fell into the quarry. All of this doesn't mean you're wrong, however. Leave me your folder and I will look into it. I promise you that."

Throughout this whole speech, the detective keeps his voice positive and light. Still, I can perceive an undercurrent of annoyance surging inside every word. He's saying whatever he needs to say to humor me so that I'll stop talking and go away. I can see behind his mask, the same way I could see behind George's. I can see in his eyes that he doesn't give a shit about Eff. He perceives her as some dreg of society simply because when he looks her up on his shitty computer, he focuses all his attention on the words "petty theft" and "drug abuse." This guy might be some magician of a detective, but he's a bad actor.

After he spews out a few more empty promises, I muster up some courage and say, "Can I speak to someone else here about this?"

"No," he says, coldly. "I'll be in touch if I learn anything new."

He shakes my hand again, squeezing slightly harder than the first time.

I leave him with my file folder, although I might as well throw it in his little mesh wastebasket, for all the good it will do. Maybe I'm being too negative. Maybe for his next trick, the World's Greatest Magician Detective will actually investigate the cult and figure out what really happened to Eff. Right.

Half an hour later, I'm shivering in the ICU waiting room. The fabric of my button-down is too thin. I could easily drive to the motel and rest for a while before visiting hours even begin, but I don't feel like making the effort. And, to be honest, part of me wants to experience some discomfort right now. Eff shouldn't have to suffer alone.

Nearby, a little girl in pigtails feeds pretzel after pretzel to the hippo puppet on her father's hand.

"That's enough," the father says. "I can't eat another bite."

"Just one more," she says.

"Okay."

As the puppet chews, the crumbs plummet onto the faux-wood floor. When the puppet's finished, he lets out a long, almost inaudible burp, and the girl laughs. The father then looks at me with an apologetic look. I reply with a smile.

The smart thing would be for me to strike up a conversation with this father and daughter. I could tell the girl that I'm a princess sometimes. I could tell her about my rabbit puppet Mr. Velvet, who sings about his dreams of hopping over the Empire State Building and Mount Everest and the moon. I could sing her Mr. Velvet's song, in Mr. Velvet's voice, if she insists. Talking to this girl would keep my mind off things, if only I could find the will to speak.

Instead, I stare at a faux knot in the faux-wood floor, and I think about the night Eff fell. Every time I imagine what happened to her, I add more details. There's nothing I enjoy more than torturing myself, I guess. This time, I see her wandering alone in a forest of ponderosa pines and incense cedars and white firs. She's wearing a boho maxi dress with a floral print, or maybe a tie-dye t-shirt with *MAY THE QUARTZ BE WITH YOU* printed in purple cursive on the front. I can smell the Evan Williams Black Label on her breath. As she hikes in the moonlight, she brushes her fingertips against leaves and branches and pine needles. Every so often, she takes a long drag on her vape pen, tasting some spiritual-sounding flavor, like elderberry or white sage.

"Tell me all your secrets," she whispers, staring up at the full moon.

The moon doesn't respond to her, so she moves on.

At one point, she trips on a tangled root and breaks her fall with her hands. After standing again, she pulls a pine needle out of her left palm. She doesn't really mind. She can hardly feel the pain at this point.

Eventually, she finds herself standing at the edge of an abandoned quarry. Is it still called a quarry if it has nothing left to give, or is it now merely a hole in the world? In any case, the quarry looks to her like an amphitheater dug into the ground, with rows of stone seats descending from the perimeter. These seats are massive, and fit only for giants, and so Eff pictures an audience of cyclopes and dragons and gargantuan trolls. Maybe she imagines herself at the bottom of the quarry, singing a Celine Dion song into an oversized microphone for the giants. This is the sort of thing she would describe, anyway, if I were standing at the edge of the quarry with her.

Suddenly, the ground crumbles below Eff's feet. She lets out a bewildered gasp, or possibly she doesn't make any sound at all. For a while, she tumbles down a slope of dirt, grasping wildly for anything to hold onto. And then the slope grows impossibly steep, and she drops straight down. She falls, and falls. Finally, her body slams onto sliced stone. Bones shatter. Her consciousness scampers away to some dark hiding spot, away from all this pain. A jagged rock protrudes from her left thigh, but at least she can't feel that at the moment. For who-knows-how-long, she lies there on one of the giant's seats, slowly dying, until someone finds her.

This is the version of events Detective Burns would have me believe. Eff was walking in the dark too close the quarry and the ground crumbled under her and she fell.

In another version, Eff's walking through the forest with a man at her side. She's wearing the maxi dress with a floral print and a burnt-orange pleather jacket. She doesn't need the jacket, but the fabric feels a little like armor over her skin. I can detect the whiskey on her breath. She doesn't believe she can do this sober.

The two of them walk deeper and deeper into the forest. Eff doesn't brush her fingertips against the trees. She keeps her arms crossed over her chest. From time to time, she glances at the man beside her.

"I need to talk with you about something," Eff says.

"So you said," the man says. Let's call him Fredrick. I knew a Fredrick in elementary school who enjoyed pulling my hair.

Eff stops walking. "I'm worried about you, Fred. I'm worried about your soul." She bites at the nail of her pinky finger. "First you joke around about finding George and breaking his legs, and then you disappear for a few days."

"I was getting supplies," Frederick says.

Eff says, "And I believed you for a while. But then my

sister sent me this. George was in a hit-and-run." She pulls my letter out of her jacket pocket. She holds out the photo of George with the chasmic gash from his nose to his ear.

Frederick waves away the photo with a trembling hand. "Whatever happened to your ex has nothing to do with me. I was getting supplies. Really."

Eff shakes her head. "I wish I could believe that, Fred. But I've been having visions, even before I learned about George. I've seen the hit-and-run at least a dozen times. Over and over, I've experienced George's terror and his pain. I wanted to believe the whole vision thing was some bullshit my mind was coming up with, but now I know it really happened. You did it, Fred."

The man stares at a pine cone in front of his right foot. "I did it for you," he says, almost in a whisper.

"You might have convinced yourself of that, but that's not true. In the visions, I connected with your spirit as well as George's. I felt your giddiness when you ran him over. When you looked at the rearview mirror and you saw his body, you laughed." She takes a step closer to Fredrick. She wants to put a hand on his shoulder, but she's too nervous to do so. Instead, she bites at her fingernail again. "Anyway, like I said, I'm worried about you. We're supposed to be here to find our best selves. Suffice it to say, you're heading down the wrong path. You need help, Fred. We need to talk to someone about what happened."

Maybe this is when Fredrick panics. Maybe this is when he realizes where they are, and he pushes her off the edge of the forest.

Once again, I picture her tumbling, and grasping, and falling. I hear the cacophony of snaps as her body collides with the stone. Her consciousness implodes.

High above her, Fredrick uses a pointy stone to hack away at the edge of the quarry. Chunks of earth hail onto her ragdoll of a body. Fredrick hopes that this will be enough to deceive the police. They'll believe the ground collapsed under her, and they won't investigate any further because Eff isn't worth their time. Eff is a nobody, he believes. No one in the world cares about her.

This whole scene comes across as absurd while it plays through my head. The dialogue doesn't seem very realistic. Eff hardly sounds like herself. Nevertheless, there could be some truth here. There's a chance Eff confronted Fredrick, or whatever his real name is, because of my letter. There's a chance he, or multiple cultists, attempted to kill her.

I jump a little when the little girl in pigtails materializes in front of me.

"Do you want one?" she says, holding a pretzel stick between two small fingers.

"It's not one that fell on the floor," the father says.

"Oh thank you," I say, in a slightly princessy voice.

Grinning, the girl returns to her seat. Once again, I almost tell her about my dress and my magic wand and my rabbit puppet. And once again, I don't. The girl goes back to playing with her father, and I hold the pretzel stick in my hand, like a sort of good luck charm. I'm going to need all the luck I can get really.

The world doesn't give a shit about Eff, so it's up to me to investigate the cult and figure out what happened to her. They can't hide from me now. I know their name. As I wait for visiting hours, I use my phone to look up everything I can find on the Merry Dredgers and their retreat. There isn't much information out there beyond a barebones website packed with esoteric nonsense. There aren't any pictures of them or the retreat. There aren't any names of individuals. But apparently they operate a booth at a local farmers' market every week here in Lonbloom.

I keep reading. I keep searching. After a while, the man

and his daughter walk out of the room, and I check the time on my phone. Visiting hours have already started. I know I need to go, but I don't want to go back there. I don't want to see my sister's mutilated face or my father's sunken eyes. My heart beats fast. My ribs feel as if they're contracting, squeezing everything inside them like talons. I need a few minutes to calm myself. So for a while, I focus my attention back on the Dredgers and my schemes and the currents of rage surging through my limbs. Maybe I shouldn't feel the way that I'm feeling, but I don't care. Eff deserves justice, doesn't she? I'm going to find these bastards and I'll do whatever it takes to make them pay.

FOUR

A few days later, and I'm zigzagging my way down a bustling pedestrian street. I purchase a popcorn ball decorated with candy googly eyes and peruse a stall selling crocheted bigfoots and moth men and chupacabras. I would probably buy one, if not for the fact that I have very little money, and I have an investigation to finance. A few yards down from the amigurumi, a sweaty man in a Hawaiian shirt and a white fedora paces in front of a white folding table with a small speaker dangling from his belt. "Charles Darwin was a reptilian demon," he bellows into his headset. "He was sent to Earth by Beelzebub himself. The evidence is right here in Darwin's lost diaries." I glance at the pyramid of books on his folding table. The cover of the book features an illustrated Darwin sitting cross-legged atop a giant, horned tortoise. Surprisingly enough, this guy isn't one of the cultists. Farther down the street, a boy rides a pony in a small circle, wearing an adult-size cowboy hat that covers his eyes. "I'm a horse guy," he yells, over and over.

I'm not actually hungry after that gigantic popcorn ball, but that doesn't stop me from waiting in line for street tacos and Diet Coke. At this point, I'll do anything to delay the inevitable. Hell, I'm considering going back and chatting with the sweaty preacher, or whatever he is.

Despite my best efforts, I eventually find myself approaching my destination. I take a deep breath. I tell myself that this is simply another performance. I push away the cynical, standoffish Seraphina. Picture me dressed in sunset-colored robes or an all-black tracksuit or a prairie dress that stretches down to my ankles. I need to smile easily. I need to trust easily. I need to be more like Eff.

At booth twelve, I find a few small tables loaded with glittery green cupcakes and patchwork jackets and windchimes made from colorful sea glass. One of the tables showcases a cluster of intricately carved, painted candles. A particular candle catches my eye, depicting a tuxedo cat sitting on an unkempt lawn, holding a garden glove in his mouth.

"Hello," I say, in a voice that sounds like a cross between my princess and my regular voice. I put on a smile that feels artificial, as if I'm wearing wax lips.

The old guy behind the table looks up at me, holding a small knife in his hand.

"Hi there," he says.

Suddenly, I can't remember any of the possible lines of dialogue that I came up with for this moment. I'm quite the spy, aren't I?

"These are interesting candles," I say, motioning to the objects, as if he might not know which candles I'm referring to. "Are you the artist?"

"Nah," he says. "I'm afraid I don't have an artistic bone in my body. These belong to Nichelle. She's off powdering her nose or some such, but she should be back any second." He rubs his thumb over his bushy mustache, like some cartoon villain. "All I know about the candles is that they contain certain magical properties. I'm afraid I know less about magic than I do about art. You'll have to ask Nichelle when she comes back."

"Okay," I say. I'm nothing if not a brilliant conversationalist.

The man then abandons me to help another customer, so I return my attention to the candles. Next to the tuxedo cat, there's a candle that depicts an anthropomorphic spoon wearing a pinstripe suit, standing on the surface of the moon. The candle beside that one depicts a torchlit tunnel behind a sliding bookcase.

"This young lady was asking about your candles," the old guy says, causing me to jump a little.

I look up and see a young woman wearing a black, crew-neck t-shirt and a gold necklace with a wooden moon pendant. She gives me a very realistic smile that puts my counterfeit grin to shame. I almost feel guilty for deceiving her. I squeeze two fingers of my left hand with my right.

"Is there any particular candle you're drawn to?" she says, quietly.

I take a step forward and say, "The tuxedo cat."

She reaches out and picks up the candle in question. "This is Doctor Pepper," she says. "He was my childhood cat. He used to steal things from the neighbors' yards, like garden gloves and dog toys. You like cats?"

"Yeah," I say. If I'm going to accomplish my mission, I need to stop speaking in monosyllabic sentences. I need to make a connection here. "I have a cat named Athena," I lie. "She's no neighborhood thief, but she does sometimes steal my socks and carry them to her cat bed."

"That's so cute," Nichelle says.

"You haven't heard the cutest part yet. She likes to sleep with the sock as her pillow."

"Alright, yeah. That's painfully cute. I might die from the cuteness."

At this point, Nichelle carefully returns the candle to the table. Her nail polish brings to mind an abalone shell.

"So what do these candles do exactly?" I say. "A little, mustachioed birdy told me they have magical properties."

"Yep," she says. "They're pretty much chock-full of positive vibes. I used to inscribe my candles with magical symbols and words of power and whatnot, but nowadays I carve whatever images make me happy."

"Spoons wearing pinstripe suits make you happy?" I say.

"One particular spoon does, yes," she says. "He showed up in one of my dreams a few weeks ago. He was a stand-up comedian. I can't remember any of his jokes, but he was legitimately funny. My roommate told me I was laughing my head off in my sleep. Don't look at me like that. It's not that weird."

"I'm not judging," I say.

Nichelle sighs. "No matter what you think, they are effective candles. Cecil, didn't my candle help you out? Cecil?"

"What?" the old guy says, slicing a tomato with his pocketknife.

"Didn't my candle help you out last week?"

"I suppose it might have," he says, and uses his knife to convey a sliver of tomato into his mouth.

Nichelle sighs again.

"I believe you," I say. "And magic aside, they're beautiful candles. I love the cat. Even the spoon guy is lovely in an Al Capone sort of way."

She stares at me silently for a few moments, biting her lip. Then she says, "You can have the cat, if you want. For free, I mean. You seem drawn to him."

"Oh no," I say. "I'll buy him for the regular price."

"There is no regular price." She grabs the cat candle and begins wrapping her creation in brown paper. "I give them away to whoever needs them. You're drawn to the cat, so he might do you some good." She carefully places the wrapped-up candle in a gift bag. Printed on the front of the bag is a Humpty Dumpty statue with a crack in his skull. He grins at me, viciously.

"Thank you," I say.

When she hands me the candle, her finger brushes against my hand. Did she do that on purpose?

Nichelle tucks a loose lock of hair back behind her ear and says, "You should come back next week and tell me how everything goes with Doctor Pepper. I'd recommend burning him during the full moon."

"Okay," I say, but to be honest, there's no way I'm burning this candle. I already know that for sure. And it's not that I'm afraid of the magic I might unleash, because this candle holds no more power than my foam princess wand. But I'm not about to destroy a piece of artwork that someone put so much work into, even if she is a cultist. This is the reason I can't watch those shows where bakers spend six hours decorating a cake to look like a mermaid and then slice her up as soon as they're finished.

"I'm Nichelle, by the way," she says.

"I already told her your name," Cecil says, stabbing a bell pepper.

"I'm Corinna," I say.

Nichelle reaches out to me, and I notice speckles of paint on her palm and forearm. I shake her hand.

"See you next week," she says.

Is this the standard operating procedure for these people? They give you a candle and touch your hand and then ask to see you again so they can keep the conversation going? I'm sure they use Nichelle as a recruiter because she's pretty and easy to talk to. Nothing about her feels sinister in any way.

Is this what happened to Eff? Was she given a candle as well?

"Are you alright?" Nichelle says.

"Yeah," I say. "Thanks again for Doctor Pepper."

Once again, I'm picturing Eff at the quarry, and I can feel

a tangled mass of emotions burgeoning in my chest. I can feel myself losing control.

I walk away.

That night, with Heracles purring on my lap, I consider lighting up the candle out of a sense of vengeance. The Dredgers almost killed my sister. Why shouldn't I destroy their artwork? They deserve that, and more.

"Sorry, Hare," I say, and the cat bites gently at my hand as soon as I lift him off my lap.

I almost light the candle using the barbeque lighter above the fridge, but I stop myself. Instead, I search the junk drawer for the matchbook Eff sent me a few years ago with the go-go dancer on the cover.

I use one of Eff's matches to light up the candle. A feeling of righteousness washes over me, but then the wave recedes and all I can think about is poor Doctor Pepper melting away to nothingness.

The days rush by in a blur and Eff doesn't get any better, but at least she doesn't get any worse. When I'm outside of the hospital, I tell myself stories about Eff waking up, and sometimes she's her same old self, and sometimes she's different. When I'm inside the hospital, all my stories flee from me like frightened rabbits. When I look at my sister in the harsh florescent light of reality, I feel certain she's going to die. I feel certain that I'm going to lose the last human being in the world I truly love and who truly loves me. I already lost my father, and I lost Aunt Gloria, but I guess that's not enough for the universe, is it? Someday soon, I'm going to be thoroughly alone.

When I'm sitting beside Eff, I also like to chastise myself for not spending enough time with her the past many years. I went months sometimes without texting her. I didn't want to bother her during her many adventures. I didn't want to be a nuisance in her life. But I should have reached out more often, and we should have hung out more often. During those rare occasions when we did spend time together in person, she would open her heart to me and tell me everything, and I wouldn't do the same. She probably felt bad about that. I know she did. I don't know what's wrong with me.

Outside of the hospital, I continue working parties and feeding dogs. Also, I set up a fundraiser on a crowdfunding site, asking for money so that I can take some time off to care for my sick sibling. It's sort of the truth, I guess. I use my princess profiles on social media to signal boost the fundraiser. I have a lot of followers. Nevertheless, even by day seven, I haven't made much money at all.

Sometimes I almost call Alvin to tell him about Eff, but I don't want to bother him. We've drifted apart the past year or so, and I'm sure he's happier this way. All I ever did was frustrate him and weigh him down.

Sometimes when I'm dreaming, I realize that I'm dreaming and I look for Eff. I shout her name. I can never find her.

A week after my first visit I'm back at the farmers' market. The sweaty guy with the headset is even sweatier than last time. He booms, "Darwin kept a pet tortoise in a basement after he returned to England. He fed the reptile nothing but pig entrails. Sometimes Beelzebub would enter the tortoise's body and give Darwin special instructions." Nearby, four ponies clomp around in a small circle without any children on their backs.

At booth twelve, I once again find Cecil and Nichelle. This time around, Nichelle's dressed in black floral-print shorts and a white halter top. She's wearing a gold necklace with a black opal pendant. As she chats with a customer, she turns a red bell pepper over and over in her hands. Her opal sparkles in the sunlight when she moves.

Eventually, she notices me. "It's you," she says, smiling.

"This is terrible, but the second after you told me your name, I forgot. I'm terrible with names."

For a second, I can't remember the fake name I came up with. "I'm Corinna," I say.

"Corinna Corinna Corinna Corinna Corinna Corinna Corinna. That should do it."

"Are you sure you said it enough times?"

"Ha ha," she says, and she balances the bell pepper on top of a tomato. "So how'd it go with the candle? Did you burn him?"

"Yeah," I say. In actuality, I blew out the candle ten seconds after lighting it. I didn't have the heart to destroy Doctor Pepper.

"Great," she says. "Did it do you some good, do you think? Did you notice any changes in your life?"

"I . . . the day after I burned the candle, someone gave me a hundred-dollar tip. Also, my car's been screeching at me for the past I-don't-know-how-many days, so I took it into the shop. It turns out I only needed to get a brake pad replaced. They didn't even try to upsell me for once." There are kernels of truth in what I'm saying. Someone did give me a generous tip the other day, although it was for forty dollars. And my car is still screeching.

"That's great," Nichelle says, beaming. "I'm so glad to hear that."

"I really can't thank you enough," I say, as earnestly as I can manage. "Beyond the good luck, I've felt so much calmer the past few days. My life's been a bit chaotic lately, so it was nice to—" This is where I make my voice break. Then I picture Eff lying on her hospital bed, her face a web of tubes and cuts and bruises. I make myself cry.

"Are you alright?" Nichelle says, rushing around the folding table. "Of course you're not alright. What am I saying?"

I wipe away my tears with a fingertip.

"Can I get you anything?" she says, tall and blurry beside me.

"No," I say. "I'm fine. Thank you."

"Are you sure? I could get us some aguas frescas. Or I could buy you a soda. I don't drink soda myself, but I don't mind buying you one."

"An agua fresca would be good."

"Alright. I'll be right back."

We end up sitting together on a bench underneath a magnolia tree. As I sip the agua fresca, the taste of strawberry blends with the spicy-lemon scent of the magnolia flowers.

"I'm sorry about whatever you're going through," Nichelle says. "I know we don't know each other or anything, but you can tell me about it if you want."

Nearby, two boys who could be brothers arm wrestle on the grass. The older brother keeps tapping the younger brother on the head with his free hand. I watch them and say, "My father passed away recently. He died from lung cancer. He didn't smoke a day in his life, but the universe didn't seem to care." This isn't what killed my dad when I was a kid, but it's close enough to cause me pain.

"I'm so sorry," Nichelle says. "Can I give you a hug?"

"Okay."

Leaning to her side, Nichelle wraps one arm around me and squeezes gently. After a second, she pulls her body away.

"He was such a kind person," I say, my voice breaking for real this time. I can see my father's squinty smile. I can see his freshly polished black oxfords. I can see him snapping dorkily to the radio. "He didn't deserve to die like that."

"You're right," she says. "He didn't."

I want Nichelle to believe that I'm grieving, but maybe I shouldn't have mentioned my father. This doesn't feel like a performance anymore. I feel too much like a little girl again, trapped in my giant coffin, surrounded by enormous worms. I need to regain control of myself.

As I sip at my agua fresca, the two boys kick their flip-flops high into the air.

I can feel Nichelle looking at the side of my head.

After a while, she says, "I've lost loved ones before. What helped me was being around kind people. I don't know if you're in need of more people, but if you are, you can come hang out with me and my friends this weekend."

I look at her.

She continues, "Right now, I'm living at this spiritual retreat. It's really cool. We're hosting a wedding there for a couple of our members this weekend, so that should be cute. I don't drink, but there'll be an open bar with a signature cocktail and everything. What do you think? Would you want to go?"

A droplet of sweat slithers down my back. I know I should tell her no. I know that visiting the headquarters of the Dredgers would probably be the worst mistake of my life.

"Sure," I say, grinning like a thick-witted princess who's about to eat a poisonous apple. "That sounds fun."

FIVE

During the three-hour drive to the so-called retreat, I keep picturing a wild-eyed man in ceremonial robes breaking my legs or dumping my body down a well or shoving me off the edge of a quarry. I picture myself tumbling, and grasping, and falling. To distract my mind, I listen to a podcast about a man who would break into wealthy women's homes and sleep curled up in a closet or under a bed. He would chew up feathers in his mouth and spit them out inside random drawers throughout the home. As a rule, true crime stories calm me down somehow, but not today.

Eventually, I turn my thoughts to Eff. I remember this chilly afternoon in the park when our spaceship crash-landed on some lush planet with singing gardenias. We could see our breath every time we exhaled, and we pretended that each little cloud of condensation was a wisp of our souls leaving our bodies. With each breath, we lost more and more. We forgot words. We forgot how to walk, and we had to crawl around on the damp grass. We begged the flowers to help us, but they only sang about how we were doomed. Like always, our mother came to get us from the park before we could finish our story. We were upset to leave, but on our walk back home, Eff told me not to worry because she knew exactly where we could find our missing soul chunks.

At home, I followed her to her room and she crawled under her bed and dragged out the wooden box Aunt Gloria gave her with the puppy painted on the top. Inside the box, there was an ancient piece of cotton candy. She gave me half. I was slightly disgusted by the look of the candy, but I ate it, and we pretended that all the missing pieces of ourselves came rushing back. "I remember how to talk," I said. "I remember how to walk," she said.

As soon as I park my car, I look through my purse for the pepper spray I purchased yesterday. Yes, I still have it. The bottle didn't magically leap out of my bag during the drive here. How the pepper spray is supposed to help protect me against an entire cult, I have no idea.

For a few moments, I sit silently in my car. Eff always likes to talk about the crossroads moments in a person's life, and this definitely feels like one of those. I can still turn back. I can drive home to Heracles and my Netflix queue and the mint chocolate chip ice cream in the freezer. This is your last chance, Seraphina.

I exit my car.

The first thing my eyes are drawn to is the colossal, puke-green face towering in front of me. He has three sunken eyes and lumpy skin and a sharp-edged nose. Each of his fangs is a different color. The green paint of his face flakes and peels and cracks, as if the creature is in the process of shedding his skin. Faded, jagged letters on his forehead spell out the words *oblintropolis USA*. I'm guessing there's a G in front of *oblintropolis* that's too faint for me to see. As I watch, the creature's yellow eyes shift to the left and then the right.

According to Nichelle's handwritten directions, in order to enter the retreat, I can simply "walk through the front door."

I approach the giant, brutish visage. I wish there were a spyhole I could peek through before entering, but the place is surrounded by a medieval-looking wall made of imitation stone. Three-eyed monsters glare at me through the gaps in the battlements, pointing crossbows in my general direction. After checking for my pepper spray one last time, I close the distance between myself and the wooden door centered in the goblin's mouth. The door's inscribed with hundreds of overlapping circles and triangles and other more irregular geometric figures. I'm probably just carsick after my long drive, but as my focus moves from shape to shape to shape, I start to feel a little dizzy.

The doorknob's shaped like a cluster of brass eyes. Maybe if the door is locked, I should turn around and go home and forget about this whole horrible scheme. But the doorknob turns. I try to pull the door at first, but it doesn't budge, so I push instead.

Once I'm swallowed up and inside the compound, I tell myself to calm down. I haven't even spoken to anyone yet, and I'm already sweating like that preacher from the farmers' market. The perspiration feels like cold, wet fingers grazing my back. I leave the door open, in case I need to make a quick escape.

Nichelle promised to meet me here at the entrance, but she's nowhere to be seen.

To my right, a roller coaster train rests upside-down on the cracked pavement. The front of the train features a rusty, grinning wolf's head wearing a crown. I spot a dead rat with an open mouth lying on the ground next to the wolf's head, and this brings to mind some nightmare I can only half-remember. To my left, I'm confronted with a looming, cylindrical structure made of the same artificial stones I saw outside. Fake vines as thick as my thighs strangle the tower, speckled with dozens of brownish-yellow flowers. In the center of each wilted flower, there's a bulbous, amphibious-looking eye.

"The Keep," I mumble to myself, reading the wooden sign above the tower door. Unlike the rollercoaster and everything else around me, the Keep appears freshly painted and immaculately maintained.

I wait for Nichelle. As time passes, I become more and more positive that I'm not here for a wedding. Who would have a wedding in some fucked-up amusement park? Any minute now, the door in the goblin's mouth is going to slam shut and they'll bar it from the outside. They'll grab me and tie me up and toss me into their sacred quarry where they throw all their sacrifices. I need to stop thinking like this, because my eyes are tearing up. I feel dizzy. I have to stop freaking out. Through my watery eyes, I notice someone with a wide frame standing at the top of the tower. I can't make out his features, but he seems to be staring straight ahead. With every passing moment, he steps closer and closer to the edge of the battlement. I know I should yell for him to stop, but my body won't obey me. I manage to reach a useless, trembling hand in his direction.

He jumps. And he drifts downward, as if in slow motion. Is he actually drifting, or am I perceiving time in some wonky way? I wipe my eyes. As soon as he hits the checkered pavement, his body shatters. His arms detach. His torso splits down the middle and the two halves topple over in opposite directions.

"He does that every hour," Nichelle says, somewhere behind me.

In a miracle of engineering, the body parts of the fallen figure draw together and reassemble. Whole once again, Humpty Dumpty zips upward, faster than he fell, and then he disappears from view.

"Are you alright?" Nichelle says, at my side now.

My mouth feels dry, as if I've just tossed back a shot glass full of sand.

Finally, I manage to say, "I'm good."

"Sorry I'm late," Nichelle says. "I lost track of time."

"It's fine," I say.

With some effort, I manage to turn my attention away from the Keep. Nichelle's dressed in a shimmery black top and a black circle skirt speckled with white-and-red flowers. As before, she's wearing a gold necklace. Today, a flame-shaped pendant tugs at the chain.

"So, are you ready to meet everyone?" she says. "The wedding's in the Haunted Forest. It's not as creepy as it sounds."

"Okay," I say.

We walk in silence for a while, weaving our way through dead, blackened weeds growing through the many cracks in the pavement.

Nichelle clears her throat and says, "You probably think this is a weird place for a retreat."

"Oh no," I say. "Most retreats and spas I've gone to have been located inside creepy, abandoned amusement parks."

Nichelle laughs softly. "Ernie's a pretty eccentric guy," she says. "He's the owner of this place. When he was a kid, he constantly fantasized about living in an amusement park, so this retreat is a literal dream come true. I'm sure once you meet him, you'll hear the whole story. He loves telling it."

If Ernie owns this place, does that mean he's the leader? When I scoured the Merry Dredgers' website, I couldn't find any mention of a particular prophet or leader they follow, but that doesn't mean there isn't one.

We continue forward, and as the sun descends behind us, the shadows of the park lengthen and contort. We approach a corroded carousel populated by red-eyed rabbits with golden wings. Huge stuffed animals straddle most of the rabbits. I see a green Spongebob Squarepants with muscular arms and a Mario without a mustache and a Teletubby with the face of a gorilla. These bootleg toys make me feel as if I've wandered into some alternate dimension only slightly different from our own.

A statue of one of the three-eyed goblins stands near the carousel with his arm outstretched. When Nichelle passes by the monster, she gives him a leisurely high five. Wherever I look, I see statues of these three-eyed fiends frozen in various poses. There's one dangling a giant cockroach over his open mouth. There's two of them about to punch each other in the face. Why do all the goblins have three eyes and multicolored teeth? On second thought, why should I care?

"How's Athena?" Nichelle says.

For a second or two, I have no idea what she's talking about. Then I say, "Oh, she's good. She's stealing socks and hunting crickets. Last night she knocked my soda off the nightstand for no reason. She's living the good life."

"What a little troublemaker."

"Yeah, she's quite the scoundrel."

At this point, we turn a corner, and I get a clear view of our destination. The Haunted Forest, it turns out, is a glade made of artificial grass, partially surrounded by a semicircle of pale, barren trees. The bone-like branches bend and twist in bizarre directions. Here and there, the limbs of neighboring trees wind together in tight spirals, as if the plants are holding hands. To add to the creepiness-factor, diaphanous phantoms made of cheesecloth hang from the trees, swinging gently in the wind.

The Dredgers themselves are less creepy looking than I envisioned during my three-hour drive here. I pictured them in ceremonial robes. I pictured them naked. I pictured them in suits constructed out of raccoon heads and bird beaks. Thankfully, almost everyone's wearing dresses or dress pants and button-downs. Take away the surroundings, and this looks like any other wedding. A bearded man tosses a cocktail weenie at another man's open mouth and misses. Three women dance together, while other Dredgers chat in a circle of wicker armchairs. A woman with impressive bangs screams with laughter while pointing at someone's shoe. Something feels wrong with this picture, though, and at first I can't put my finger on what that something is. Then I realize that no one's holding a phone. No one's texting. No one's taking any pictures, except for a boyish-looking man with a bulky vintage camera.

"Maggie wanted to have drinks first thing," Nichelle says. "She said the ceremony will be less torturous this way, although they never feel like torture to me. That's Maggie over there." Nichelle waves her hand in the direction of a middle-aged woman wearing a strapless, burgundy gown with black lace over the bodice. "She's the bride, by the way. Did I mention that?"

"I don't think so," I say.

Once we step onto the artificial grass, my attention turns to a pea-soup-colored tree to my left. The branches of the tree end in scabrous hands, all closed into fists.

"I thought you said this place isn't creepy," I say, and I nod in the direction of the monstrosity.

"Alright, that tree is pretty creepy," she says. "But the rest of the Forest isn't that bad. It's pretty at night."

"If you say so."

I grab a black cocktail with a sign nearby that reads *Black Lagoon Water*. I can feel my hand shaking a little as I hold the plastic martini glass, but at least I'm calmer now than I was five minutes ago. At least they haven't tried to kill me yet. Maybe I am here for a wedding, after all. I need to think of this as just another party I'm working. I'm playing a part. I'm replacing the princess guidebook with the cultist guidebook that I spent the last few days writing in my head.

I follow Nichelle toward a small group of people, and I put on my most innocent, culty smile. Nichelle introduces me to Maggie and Surfer, her husband-to-be. Surfer's dressed in a burgundy suit and a ridiculously tall top hat.

"I love your dress," I say to Maggie.

"Thank you, sweetheart," she says, slurring her words a little. "I know we don't know each other, but I really appreciate you being here. As soon as Nichelle told me you were coming, I decided you would be my something new. All of my somethings are people. My something blue is Topher over there in that spiffy blue tux, with the hair covering his face. My something old is Cecil, but don't tell him that. You don't mind being a something, do you? I probably should have asked you first."

"I don't mind," I say. "I'd rather be treated like something than nothing."

Maggie stares at me silently for a few seconds, tilting her head a little. She says, "You know, I say you're something new, but now I get the feeling we've known each other in some other life. Can you feel that?"

"I think so," I say. I restrain the sarcastic comment that's eager to leap out of my mouth. According to the guidebook, a cultist shouldn't make fun of another cultist's ideas, no matter how absurd. I hope I can remember this.

Maggie smiles and squeezes my hand. Then she turns to Surfer. "I'm starving, sweetie."

"And what does m'lady want?" Surfer says, in a fake British accent.

"Something I'd like."

Surfer tips his top hat and races off toward the hors d'oeuvres.

"This is his final test," Maggie whispers conspiratorially. "If he gets me a quiche, I'll know that he's been paying attention to me all these years, and he'll prove his love. If he brings me anything else, I'll have to call off the wedding." She gently slaps Nichelle's arm. "I'm just kidding, Nish! You look upset. Did you think I was serious?"

Before Nichelle can reply, Surfer returns with a quiche in hand.

"See, nothing to worry about," Maggie says. "He passed with flying colors."

At this point, uplights throughout the Haunted Forest turn on simultaneously, illuminating the trees from the ground. Golden fairy lights twinkle, coiled up and down the trunks and woven through the branches. The cheesecloth phantoms also light up, glowing a pale, haunting blue. Nichelle was right. This place is pretty at night.

I'm about to express that sentiment out loud when the pea-soup-colored tree bursts into life. All over the trunk, dozens of jaundiced eyes open wide, their eyelashes thick like tarantula legs. Some of the eyes blink, and some of them leer without blinking. The mouths open next. Arranged randomly among the eyes, maws with multicolored fangs open and close, again and again, as if chanting or chewing. The polished glass teeth glimmer every time they're bared. Above, the withered hands at the ends of the branches unclench and clench, over and over.

"What the heck," Maggie says, sounding more than a little annoyed.

Cecil hustles behind the tree, limping as he moves. After a few seconds, the hands of the tree close into fists, and the mouths stop chewing, and the eyes squeeze shut.

"Phew," Maggie says, and looks over at me and Nichelle. "Me and Surfer like creepy, but the eye tree doesn't really vibe with our particular aesthetics."

"I get that," I say.

Cecil makes his way over to us. "I don't know what happened," he says. "I'm sure I turned the damned tree off this morning. Could be a faulty switch or some such. I'm sorry, Maggie."

"It's no problem," Maggie says, sounding chipper once again. "You vanquished the monster, and now all's well."

Cecil opens his mouth to reply, but instrumental music suddenly blasts at us from all sides. I don't see any speakers anywhere. They must be hidden among the artificial trees.

"Could we turn this down?" Maggie yells, in a voice that drowns out the shrieking of the pipe organ and the clanging of the piano.

After a few moments, someone somewhere brings the volume down to just above a tolerable level.

"That's better," Maggie says, and then grabs the arms of her husband-to-be. "We'd better get into position."

"Whatever you say, ma chérie," Surfer says, in a French accent that's even less believable than his British.

The two of them disappear hand-in-hand into the darkness.

"Hi again," Cecil says. "Glad you could make it."

"Thank you," I say.

With this thrilling conversation between me and Cecil at an end, we follow the rest of the guests to the center of the glade, where everyone settles onto wicker armchairs and metal folding chairs and picnic blankets. I almost throw away my plastic martini glass on the walk over, but everyone's taking their plates and glasses with them to their seats, so I do the same.

I sit on an uncomfortable metal chair, with Nichelle on my left and Cecil on my right. Cecil pulls a small green apple out of his suit jacket pocket, and a pocket knife out of the other. There aren't any apples on the hors d'oeuvre tables, so he must have brought this from elsewhere. After pulling open the pocketknife blade with his teeth, he begins peeling the apple in a long, thin strip. The sight of a cultist with a knife should probably frighten me, but the apple peeling reminds me of moments from my childhood that I actually like to remember.

"Do you want any?" Cecil says.

"No, I'm good," I say. I almost tell him about how my aunt used to peel apples the same way, but I stop myself. What if Eff told him the same thing? I need to stay vigilant here. I'm not Seraphina anymore.

I turn away from Cecil and watch as a black box near our feet coughs out a torrent of milky white vapor. Fog machines activate all throughout the Haunted Forest. The people on the blankets stand up or kneel so that they're not submerged in the miasma.

"I told them not to overdo it with the fog," Cecil says.

Before long, the wedding party strolls down the aisle toward an arch made of driftwood and burgundy-colored flowers. The flower girl cries because a woman rushes over and stops her from eating the petals. Under the arch, Surfer wipes his forehead with a grimy-looking handkerchief. He scans the audience. He winks at someone in a wicker armchair.

Once the pipe organ and piano duet fades, everyone stands, and the music is replaced by an even eerier piece, full of minor chords and dissonant sounds. I like it.

Maggie floats down the aisle, her face behind a lengthy veil of black lace. She stumbles once, and her smile only falters for a split second.

This is a cult wedding, so I half-expect the officiant to raise an ornamental dagger and ask the Great Goblin God to bless this union. I half-expect an animal sacrifice or two. Instead, the officiant talks about love and respect and dreams and the universe. He doesn't say anything I haven't heard a thousand times before. Eventually, I tune him out, and I compile a mental list of names and faces. Nichelle, Cecil, Maggie, Surfer, Topher. Ernie's the owner of the retreat, and possibly the leader. I still don't know what Ernie looks like, and that's something I need to find out. Once I get back to the car, I'll write all these names down.

As the officiant blabbers on, I search the faces of the wedding party standing on either side of the bride and groom. I search for an evil twinkle in their eye, or some indication that they might be capable of hitting George with a car and pushing my sister into a pit. I wish I did have psychic powers like Aunt Gloria believed. Maybe then I could sense the malevolence emanating for the person or people I'm searching for.

I pay attention to the ceremony again as soon as I hear Surfer speaking.

He says, "I could make a list of a hundred things I love about you. I love your freckles. I love the way you strike up conversations with random people wherever we go. I love that I can share all my thoughts and opinions with you, no matter how twisted they might be. You accept me as I am." He adds, sounding only slightly like Humphrey Bogart, "I think this is the beginning of a beautiful marriage."

Surfer wipes his forehead again, and Maggie motions for him to put the handkerchief away. Then she takes his hands.

She says, "We've known each other for ten thousand years. I'm sure everyone here can feel that. Sometimes the two of us have been brothers. Sometimes we've been mortal enemies. I'm really happy that in this lifetime, we get to be best friends. Sometimes when you kiss me, or when we're brushing our teeth, or even when we're arguing, I can hear the fates whispering in my heart. They're saying, yes, this is how you two are meant to be. This is what we planned for the two of you all along."

I can hear Nichelle sniffling beside me. When I glance over, I see the fairy lights sparkling in her eyes.

The ceremony ends with an excessively intimate kiss and the firing of way too many confetti cannons. White paper rains down on us like a blizzard. A bit of confetti lands on my arm, and I notice that the tiny piece of paper is shaped like a skull. I blast the skull away with my breath.

"This is going to be hell to clean up," Cecil says, as the wedding party tangos and salsas down the aisle.

"That was so nice," Nichelle says, smiling at me. "Don't you think?"

"Very sweet," I say, and I'm surprised that I more or less mean it.

Parched, I bring the cocktail to my lips, but I hesitate. I haven't eaten or drank anything yet tonight, because I'm mildly afraid of being poisoned or drugged. I could possibly come up with some plausible excuse for why I'm not partaking, but that might raise suspicion. I need to be part of the crowd. Everyone's eating and drinking to their heart's content, and they seem fine. I'll probably be fine.

So I take a sip. The black lagoon water tastes like vodka and some combination of fruit juices. I'm no expert, but I can't detect even a hint of arsenic.

"I hope you like pizza," Nichelle says.

"I'm a pizza maniac," I say.

Cecil nods a goodbye to us, and wanders off somewhere, dangling the apple core in front of him by the stem. As for me and Nichelle, we return to the food and drink section of the Haunted Forest. The appetizers have disappeared, and towers of pizza boxes now lean precariously on the folding tables.

"Oh no," I say. "I don't think there's enough for everyone."

"Ha," Nichelle says.

Everyone stands around the tables dumbfoundedly, because no one can reach the tops of the pizza towers. We could possibly pull a box from the bottom of the pile, but that could cause a collapse. After a few moments, long-legged creatures appear, with bodies covered with dried Spanish moss and horned faces made of bark. One of the monsters opens a pizza box and then holds out a slice to the nearest guest. I'm guessing these are people in costumes standing on stilts, unless I've somehow found myself in some circle of hell or another.

"Thank you," Nichelle says, taking a slice from one of the creatures. "Would you mind if I felt your arm?"

The monster shakes their head no and lowers an arm so that Nichelle can stroke the moss.

I take my slice and only eat a couple bites before Maggie calls me over to a small crowd near the pale trees. Once I'm close to her, she walks over and hooks her arm through mine.

"It was a beautiful ceremony," I say. "Very romantic."

"Thank you, sweetie," she says. "Did it feel preternatural?"

"Absolutely. It was definitely an otherworldly experience."

"That's exactly what we were going for," she says, almost screaming in my ear, and then she turns to Surfer. "Where's Cecil? I want a picture with all the somethings. Can somebody please find Cecil?"

I place my partially eaten pizza slice and my cocktail on a plastic chair, so that they won't be visible in the shot.

After a few seconds, someone ushers Cecil over, and the four of us somethings position ourselves around Maggie. Old, borrowed, Maggie, new, blue.

The man with the vintage camera says, "Cecil, the toothpick adds a certain raffish charm to your look, but I'm afraid toothpicks don't photograph well. Do you mind removing it? Thank you. Topher, could you move a smidge closer to our newest visitant? If she's Nichelle's friend, I'm sure she doesn't bite. Cool. Perfect. Everybody say camembert."

"Camembert," we say.

"Wait," the photographer says. "Sorry." He slightly readjusts an LED light mounted to a tripod, and then he returns to the camera. "Say camembert."

"Camembert," we say again.

We stand in silence for a few seconds before the photographer finally says, "Cool. I got it."

"Can we get one with some of the forest creatures?" Maggie says.

"You're the woman of the hour," the photographer says. "Your wish is my command."

When I pass the photographer on my way back to Nichelle, he smiles at me and says, "Enjoying yourself, Nichelle's friend?"

"Yeah," I say.

He has a boyish face, but the wrinkles around his eyes hint at his actual age. After giving me a dorky thumbs-up, he returns his attention to Maggie.

Back near the pizza towers, I find Nichelle chatting with one of the forest monsters. The creature turns out to be a circus performer and a friend of Surfer's. While tossing pizza slices to guests, the creature tells us a story about the time Surfer forced his way into a Christmas parade dressed as the grim reaper and pretended to have a heart attack. She says she can't quite remember what he meant by the performance but that it all seemed very poignant at the time.

At this point, the hidden speakers begin blasting out some upbeat, recognizable music for once.

"Come on," I say.

"I don't really dance," Nichelle says.

"That doesn't matter. I move like a possessed marionette, but I don't let that stop me."

Nichelle dances with me for a song and a half before wandering off somewhere while my back is turned.

A woman wearing a tiny top hat says, "I think it's time for the chicken dance."

"Maggie banned it," someone else says.

"Maggie's too busy to hand out punishments right now."

"Good point."

I dance, and laugh, and make a fool of myself.

After I-don't-know-how-long, I realize with a tidal wave of shame that in my efforts to blend in and socialize, I'm actually enjoying myself. I don't know why that should come as a surprise, really. After all, these people remind me of Eff and every semi-lovable, weirdo friend of hers she's introduced me to over the years. I've always liked her friends.

I walk away from the section of grass that we've adopted as a dance floor, and I remind myself that one of these people tried to kill my sister. I need to stay angry. I picture Eff in her hospital bed. She could still die because of what these people did to her. I imagine Eff in a coffin, her arms folded unnaturally over her stomach, her cuts and bruises painted over with thick makeup. Worms writhe around in the dirt around her coffin.

"Are you alright?" Nichelle says, suddenly beside me.

"I'm fine," I say, trying to sound fine, and failing miserably. "Just . . . thinking about my dad."

"I'm sorry. Can I do anything for you?"

"You could walk with me to get a water bottle. I think I'm a bit dehydrated."

In truth, I'm switching to water, because I need to stay sharp. I can't let my Corinna mask slip.

The two of us grab bottles, and as soon as we find a comfortable spot to sit down, Maggie booms, "Don't forget that we set up all the games! Surfer and Cecil worked very hard getting them ready! Now would be the perfect time to play, before we cut the cake!"

"Do you want to play some games?" Nichelle says.

"Sure," I say, standing again.

"I know a shortcut."

I follow Nichelle toward the edge of the forest. As we approach the animatronic monster tree, I notice that one of the bulging eyes glares at us, stuck in a half-open position. The tree seems otherwise dormant and non-threatening. Past the tree, we descend a set of cement steps, and everything grows dimmer and dimmer the farther we go from the forest.

Eventually we come to a colossal black wall that I can barely make out. Nichelle slides her palms against the wall, feeling for something that I can't see. After a few seconds of searching, she sighs.

"Maybe we should go back and take the long way?" I say.

"No, it's here somewhere," Nichelle says. "Give me a second. Or wait, is this the right spot?"

As soon as she finishes speaking, she opens a previously invisible door in the black wall, and I follow her inside. I find myself in a bromine-scented cave, lit by the green glow of a small exit sign. A few goblins squat nearby, frozen in time, ready to chip away at the cave wall using pickaxes. On the other side of the cave, a small wooden boat floats in a narrow stream of still, dark water. Above us, rodent-like creatures with enormous claws cling to stalactites.

We make our way past the goblins, stepping carefully over piles of round, crimson gems. I see the same gems embedded in the walls of the cave. Deeper into the tunnel, we come to a goblin squeezing and cracking open one of the gems with her bare hands. A little goblin sits inside the gem, staring up at her with large, black eyes.

Are the goblins mining for their own children? How does that work exactly? I almost ask these questions out loud, but on second thought, I don't give a shit about the life cycle of imaginary monsters.

The farther we walk, the narrower the cave becomes. After a bit, we're inching our way along a slender ledge with the cave wall on one side and the waterway on the other.

"This is narrower than I remembered," Nichelle says. "We can turn back if you want."

"No, I'm good," I say. "What's a wedding without performing at least one death-defying feat in a cave?"

As I continue sidestepping along the ledge, I see an octopus with a human face crawling on the cave wall, frozen in time like the goblins. He's strangling one of the rodent-like creatures with a barbed tentacle, his toothless mouth wide open.

Soon, the cave broadens, and we move into a battle scene. Dozens of goblins wrestle and grapple with each other, baring their jagged, multicolored teeth. They punch and kick and lift their enemies high in the air. After a few seconds, I realize that this is a party. The goblins are dancing frenetically, and drinking from painted turtle shells, and feasting on skewed tentacles and chocolate-coated cockroaches. Here and there, goblin babies sit on the shoulders of the adults, wide-eyed and grinning.

"Maggie should have invited these guys to the wedding," I say. "They look like a lot of fun."

"Yeah," Nichelle says. "You should see this place when the animatronics are running. Cecil and the others still haven't finished repairing the ride completely, but they gave me a sneak peek a few days ago. Some of the goblin babies dance a little. It's too cute."

"I can imagine."

Nichelle boops one of the babies on the nose and then she opens a door below another beaming exit sign. In a moment, we're out of the cave, facing a row of carnival games. Nichelle was right about this being a shortcut, because right now we're the only ones here.

"Which one should we play?" Nichelle says.

I scan the booths and I see one of those horse-racing games where you shoot water at a target, except with this one you're racing red-eyed rabbits with spotted wings. I see a booth with rubber eyeballs on the counter that you toss into fishbowls. One of the human-faced octopuses hangs from one tentacle above the bowls. In the next booth, there's an enormous goblin face with a few missing teeth. Near the face,

I notice a stuffed cat the size of a child. The cat's wearing rimless sunglasses and a neon windbreaker.

"Let's go for him," I say, pointing.

"Oh yay," Nichelle says. "Wait here."

She enters the booth from an opening on the side, and after a moment, she hands me a tiny metal bucket filled with beetle-shaped bean bags.

"We need to get ten teeth," she says. "If we get eight, we can get one of the smaller cats. If we get less than eight, the goblin will laugh at us and call us names."

"That's hurtful," I say.

"True, but we are trying to knock out his teeth."

"Okay, good point."

After Nichelle presses a roly-poly-shaped button on the carnival booth wall, the large goblin face comes to life. His yellow eyes cross and uncross, again and again. All his missing teeth reappear, and he begins to open and close his mouth.

"I'm going to need your help here," I say. "I'm worse at throwing than I am at dancing."

Once Nichelle returns to my side, we pelt the goblin with beetles. Every time we hit a tooth, he cackles at us as if he's enjoying this.

When we're down to one beetle, I say, "Last one. You'd better do it." I hand over the bean bag and she kisses it on the top of the head. She manages to knock out another tooth.

"My teeth!" the goblin says, with his mouth mangled and wide open. "My beautiful, magical teeth! Next time you won't be so lucky."

"How many did we get?" I say.

"Nine," Nichelle says.

"Damn it."

"Did I say we needed ten to get the big cat? I meant nine."

Moments later, Nichelle's back in the booth, handing me our furry prize.

She looks past me then and says, nonchalantly, "Hey Ernie."

I know I should turn around, but I'm suddenly terrified. I'm frozen in place like one of the goblin statues scattered around the park, destined to spend the rest of my existence smiling and cradling a giant cat like a baby.

What feels like a hundred years later, I turn to face the owner of the park.

"Hello again, Nichelle's friend." The owner, it seems, is the boyish-looking photographer from before. "So what do you think of our little operation so far?"

"It's interesting," I say. He's staring at me with an expectant look on his face. So I continue, "Nichelle said that living in a park was a childhood dream of yours."

"Oh it was definitely that," he says, and it's here that I notice the bit of spinach in his teeth. "It's an intriguing story, truly. I hope you don't mind me telling it. I promise I won't bore you."

"I won't mind."

His smile intensifies. "Cool. So five or so years ago, I was living the good life. Why don't you set that cat down? He looks heavy."

I do what he says and place the cat on the glittery counter of our carnival game. Nichelle's now standing next to me again, I notice.

"So I was living the good life," Ernie says, motioning to the right. "Let's walk."

He darts away, clicking on a small, LED flashlight. We follow him into a dark section of the park.

He continues, "I owned an 8,000 square-foot, oceanfront property with a rooftop cabana and a subterranean bar. I drove a limited-run supercar. I had a hot girlfriend whose middle name I never took the time to learn. All that to say, I was a rich asshole." On our right, we pass a ten-foot wolf standing on his back legs, howling silently at a moonless sky. The wolf's gripping a bulging burlap sack with his right hand, or paw, really. "But I was unhappy," Ernie says. "It was a frustrated, claustrophobic kind of unhappiness. I snapped at waiters. On the road, I was one of those treacherous nincompoops who weaves around traffic constantly and tailgates anyone who dares exist in front of me. I love reading with a passion, but I couldn't even finish a book in those days. Every character seemed too twee, or too irreverent, or too whatever. When a character annoyed me too intensely, I burned the novel in my firepit."

He shines a light in front of us, and I see elongated versions of ourselves with gangly limbs and malformed faces. Above the creatures, jagged letters spell out the words *Haunted Mirror Maze*. Looking glasses of various shapes and sizes decorate the building's facade. Ernie veers to the left, around the house of mirrors, away from our spindly doppelgangers. For the first time since I started following him, I think about how we're heading deeper and deeper into the compound, away from the parking lot and my car.

"I was lost," Ernie says. "I went through a phase where I read snippets of every self-help book on the planet, and I went to a hundred worthless seminars. Nothing helped for a long time. Eventually, I got into energy work, and if you're thinking, 'what the hell is that,' I don't blame you. Through energy work and meditation and other processes, I explored the labyrinth of my heart, and what I discovered there wasn't an 8,000 square-foot, oceanfront property or limited-run supercar. I came to realize that in my daily life, I was experiencing someone else's version of happiness. That's why I was so frustrated all the time."

Ernie stops suddenly, and Nichelle ends up standing on

one side of him, and I stand on the other. He shines his light forward, on a colossal face, resting sideways on the ground, with an open mouth and bulbous white mounds for eyes. As Ernie moves the flashlight to our right, I see that the face belongs to a fallen giant, tied with thick, frayed ropes to the pavement. If you wanted to, you could crawl into the giant through dozens of openings in his arm and leg and stomach.

"I came to the park often as a kid," Ernie says. "The giant was always my favorite part. I liked to believe that if you crawled through the tunnels correctly, you could find your way into the head where the treasure room was located. Maybe another kid told me that such a place existed. I can't remember." He faces me now, leaning back against the giant's featureless eye. His flashlight shines at the ground between us. He continues, "There was no treasure room, however. There was no room at all inside the head. But it was a fun idea." I can't see his face well in this light, but he seems to be looking over my shoulder, into the darkness behind me. "When I was searching for property to use as the retreat, the idea popped into my head that I should buy this place. It was a silly, stupid thought based on some absurd childhood dream, and that's why I decided to go through with it. I'm all about silly and stupid these days." He runs his hand through his hair. "So here we are, bringing this place back to life, bringing pieces of me back to life. I'm sure that sounds utterly narcissistic. But this place isn't all about me, truly. I created this retreat as a means for others to wander their own labyrinths. To use energy analysis and meditation and other processes to find out who they are, and what they want."

I can't make out Ernie's expression in this light, but I can sense that he's giving me that expectant look again. I'm sure he wants to know whether or not his little speech had the intended effect. He's charismatic, I guess, for a total blowhard. During his speech, he expressed himself with emotion and confidence, but there was also a hollowness to his words. He didn't even pretend to pause for thought. It's clear he's spoken these exact words a million times before. He could probably benefit from an acting class or two.

"That's really interesting," I say, with a sort of reverential quietness to my voice.

Ernie stares at me in silence for a few seconds. "Nichelle says that you're someone who could potentially benefit from our processes here. And I trust her judgment. And so, this is an open invitation for you to stay with us, free of charge." He holds out his hand, his palm facing me. "Now I know we're all programmed not to trust anything that's free, but I have enough money. I don't expect you to give us any kind of answer now, but think about everything I said. If you do decide to join us, I'd recommend staying at least a few weeks so that you have time enough to reap some substantial benefits from our program." He glances down at his wristwatch. "I suppose we'd better head back. I'm sure Maggie's wondering where we are."

With that, he hurries past us, and we follow a few yards behind him.

"So what do you think?" Nichelle says. "Will you come back?"

"I'm not sure yet," I lie.

"I know that everyone grieves in their own way and everything, but this place has really helped me to deal with everything. Staying here is challenging at times, but it's pretty fun overall. We're good people."

This time, when we pass the Mirror Maze, my doppelganger appears squat and wide-eyed. I must be looking into a different mirror from before.

We continue forward, and I can soon see the wolf again, howling now at a fullish moon.

"What's the wolf have in the bag?" I say.

I didn't think I was speaking loud enough for Ernie to hear me, but he says, "Goblin eggs." He slows down so that he can walk beside me. "There's a whole mythology here about the goblins and the wolf and that creepy tree, although I haven't delved too deeply into the subject. A guy named Binkler bought this park before I was born, and he's the one who transformed the place from some generic fairy tale land into Goblintropolis. He kept some of the original characters, like Humpty Dumpty and the giant. Apparently, the goblins and all the other creatures Binkler added were based on a fantasy book he wrote and never published. The manuscript was ten thousand pages long or so. I haven't read the book, but in his office, he left behind some pamphlets that summarize parts of the story. I skimmed them a few years ago."

"Interesting," I say.

"Yeah, it is that."

Once we return to the carnival games area, Nichelle says, "Oh no. The cat."

I look at the counter where we left our prize, and he's gone. I quickly scan the crowd. I can't see him anywhere. Someone must have grabbed him while we were gone.

"Maybe he needed some time alone," I say. "Maybe he's off hunting stuffed mice somewhere."

"Probably," Nichelle says.

"Well, I think I'd better head home. Thanks for inviting me. I had fun."

"I'm so glad."

I spot Maggie at the booth with the human-faced octopus, and I weave my way through the crowd surrounding her. As soon as she notices me, she smiles, a rubber eyeball in her hand.

"Are you going?" she says.

"I am," I say.

"Thank you for everything. I'm sorry we didn't have more

time to talk, but I get the feeling that we'll see each other again soon." She holds up the rubber eyeball, and using her other hand, she twirls her finger around the ball. "Our destinies are intertwined, you and me and Nichelle. I told Nichelle when I first met her that me and her were siblings in another life, and I'm starting to think you were right there with us. Does that make sense? Do you feel that?"

"Definitely," I say.

She squeezes my hand. "Surfer and I will be off on our epic honeymoon escapade soon, but I hope you're here when we come back. You and I will talk for real. You can tell me everything about everything."

"I'd like that."

Nichelle walks me back toward the front of the park, medieval-looking sconces lighting our way. Near the entrance, I see Humpty Dumpty sprawled out in fragmentary pieces on the pavement. One of his protruding eyes gazes in our direction.

"He gets stuck like that sometimes," Nichelle says. "Cecil's still working on him."

As we approach the backside of the gigantic goblin face, I notice that someone must have closed and bolted the entrance door at some point during the evening. Nichelle unbolts the door and pulls it open for me. I turn to her and she hugs me goodbye.

I walk away, out through the goblin's mouth, and Nichelle stands in the doorway, as if this is some boundary line that she shouldn't cross. After a moment, she closes the door.

As soon as I enter my car, a torrent of relief flows through me. I'm alive. I survived an infiltration into their compound. But this sense of solace doesn't last long, because on the long drive home, my damned mind's already coming up with strategies and schemes for when I come back.

SIX

A couple days later, I'm working a reptile-themed birthday party, surrounded by large inflatable snakes and lizards. I should be focusing all my energies on my princess duties, but I can't stop imagining Eff standing in a forest of pale trees and diaphanous phantoms. Sometimes Ernie pushes her into the quarry. Sometimes Surfer. Sometimes Cecil. I also keep replaying my phone conversation from this morning with one of Eff's doctors. The doctor said that Eff's condition hasn't changed. She hasn't regained consciousness. The doctor said there's still a chance Eff might recover, but I sensed an undercurrent of hopelessness in her voice.

While Mr. Velvet's singing about his dreams of leaping over the Great Pyramids, his voice breaks, and I can feel tears rushing to escape my eyes. Thankfully, during the puppet show, I'm hidden behind a collapsible, cardboard castle.

Eventually, I'm standing under the shade of a canyon live oak, crows shrieking above my head, children standing in a zigzag line in front of me.

"And what animal companion can I make for you?" I say.

The girl with smudged mermaid scales on her forehead considers for a while, staring up at the sky. "Maybe a flying sheep."

Of course, that's not on the list of animals that I gave them earlier, but I don't really care.

"A flying sheep is a wonderful choice," I say.

While I'm twisting and interconnecting the lengthy balloon into shape, I notice my phone light up, nestled on my rainbow duffle bag. I read the name.

I quickly finish up the flying sheep, and hand over what looks like a balloon dog.

"He doesn't got any wings," the girl says.

"They're very delicate and very magical. If you look carefully, you can see them glistening. Can you see them now?"

She holds the balloon over her head and squints at her new companion. "Yeah. I can."

I make a show of looking into my duffle bag. "Oh no. The rascally badger has taken all my balloons! But don't worry. I have more in my carriage. I'll return in a few short minutes. Can you all wait patiently for me?"

"Yeah," a few of the kids say, almost simultaneously.

I walk over to the birthday girl's mom and whisper, "Sorry about this. I'll be right back."

"It's fine," the woman says, way louder than a whisper.

I grab my phone and my bag and dash away. This morning, I texted Alvin and asked him to call me. I told him I need a favor. I'm dreading this conversation, but I need to get it done. Once I'm out of the yard, I call Alvin back. I'm still walking when he picks up. He initiates a video chat.

"Hi," I say.

"No offense," Alvin says. "You look completely grotesque. Some of your princess looks are cute, and you yourself are a gorgeous human being, but this reptilian princess thing you have going on is monstrous."

"Okay, shut up."

He grins at me. "I feel like we haven't spoken to each other in six months. What's wrong with us?"

"I don't know." I don't tell Alvin that me drifting apart from a friend isn't some anomaly in my life. I could teach a master class on the subject for advanced loners.

"So catch me up," Alvin says. "Please tell me you've been auditioning again."

"Not really. Not for a long time. Hold on."

I slide into the passenger seat of my jalopy and start up the car. I crank up the air conditioning to full blast. Once I'm semi-comfortable, I tell Alvin about what happened to Eff, or at least some version of the truth that doesn't involve a cult.

After his outpouring of sympathy, I say, "Eff's in a hospital up north, and I'm hoping to stay with her for a week or two. I need someone to watch Heracles when I'm away."

"Sure I'll watch him," Alvin says, waving off my worries. "I love that little hairball."

"Thank you." The thought of inconveniencing Alvin further makes me nauseous, but I don't have a large list of people I can turn to. "There's another thing I wanted to ask you. Like I said, I'm hoping to head up north for a while, and I wondered if I could borrow a little money. I'm broke, and these app jobs don't give me any paid time off." I've raised some money through my online fundraiser, but not enough. I tell him how much I need.

Alvin's silent for a moment. He says, "Of course I'll help you, Phina. And stop feeling bad about asking me. I can see it in your face, even under that demonic makeup. I'll talk with Anton. I'm sure he'll agree we can spare a little something. We're not hurting for cash these days."

"Thank you, Alvin. Well, I need to get back. We need to catch up for real soon."

After one last deluge of sympathy, he says goodbye and I head back toward the party. Alvin told me not to feel bad about asking for money, but that's easier said than done. I could teach a master class in guilt as well.

I struggle my way through two more parties, and now I'm in bed, with Heracles curled up on his bee-print pillow beside me. The good thing about being this exhausted is that my insomnia doesn't quite manage to keep me awake all night.

Once I close my eyes, I'm back in the ICU waiting room. I scan the area for any signs of life. Crumpled-up papers and empty chip bags speckle the faux-wood floor. Someone should really clean this place up. This can't be hygienic.

I'm here, of course, because Eff wrote me a letter and said that she's kept her baby inside her for too long. Labor should have been induced long ago, but Eff avoided going to the hospital until today.

With nothing better to do, I pick up a crumpled-up piece of paper from the waiting room floor and attempt to place the trash into my duffle bag. I say attempt because before I can accomplish my good deed, Heracles reaches a paw out of my bag and bats the ball of paper out of my hand.

"Hare," I say. "You're making a mess."

I hear some soft footsteps in the hallway, and I assume that it's a doctor or nurse coming to update me on Eff's condition. Instead, a baby steps into the waiting room, coated with a thin layer of slime, wobbling like a baby deer walking for the first time.

"Seraphina," she says, in a weak, high-pitched voice.

I study her carefully. She looks a little like Eff did as a child, with her droopy, chunky cheeks, and her saucer eyes. The only real difference is that this baby's limbs seem much too thin, and her eyes and nose and mouth seem slightly out of place.

"Seraphina," she says again, stepping forward.

For the first time, I notice the broken pieces of multicolored glass on the floor. They're hidden among the crumpled-up papers and chip bags and banana peels. I spot a few dead gophers curled up among the trash, their long incisors bent in bizarre directions.

"Stay right there," I say.

The baby's not listening to me. She's still floundering forward on wobbly legs. I can see that she's already stepped on some glass because she's leaving a trail of bloody footprints behind her. If she steps on one of the gophers, what kind of disease might she contract?

And so, I rush forward and pick her up in my arms. She feels lighter than she looks. She's as tall as a five-year-old but she has barely any flesh on her at all.

She wraps her arms around me, and I hug her, careful not to squeeze her too tight.

"You're okay now," I say.

She must have wandered off from Eff's delivery room while Eff was asleep. They probably didn't expect the baby to be able to walk so soon after being born.

I carry her out of the waiting room.

"We'll find your mom," I say, peering down the impossibly long, stark hallway. Before I can take another step, the baby begins to melt in my arms, flailing and screaming. I can hear Eff yelling in a hospital room far away.

SEVEN

Nichelle meets me at the entrance to Goblintropolis where I left her four days ago. She's wearing a tucked-in top with short, embroidered sleeves, and the same black floral-print shorts I've seen before. Today, her pendant's in the shape of a spoon.

Pointing for a second at her necklace, I say, "Hey, is that in honor of the spoon comedian from your dream?"

"Yep," she says. "It's so cute, right?"

I enter the goblin's mouth and Nichelle bolts the door behind us. The two of us walk side-by-side into the park. On my right, I spot someone wearing a goblin mask and yellow work pants with reflective bands below the knees. With one hand, he's wheeling around a propane tank strapped to a hand truck, and with the other, he's holding a blowtorch.

As soon as he spots us, he waves.

I let go of my rolling suitcase and wave back.

"That's Topher," Nichelle says.

I remember him from the wedding. He was Maggie's something blue.

I say, "No judgment, but why exactly is he going around in a goblin mask with a blowtorch?"

Nichelle laughs and says, "He's burning weeds. As for why he's wearing the goblin mask, I have no clue. We found the masks in storage recently. Ernie says that when he was a kid, the park staff would wear them during the Halloween season to scare the guests."

I watch as Topher burns a patch of dandelions to a crisp.

Nichelle continues, "Topher and Surfer used to do performance art together. They're both pretty theatrical."

We leave Topher to his work, and head toward the massive cylindrical tower. Near the entrance of the Keep, Cecil's sitting cross-legged on the pavement, wearing a woven garden hat, tinkering with the fractured Humpty Dumpty.

"Hi again," he says. "Glad you decided to come back."

"Thanks," I say.

Nichelle taps the point of her shoe against a piece of Humpty's shell. "How's the patient?" she says. "Is he feeling any better?"

"Nah, not really." Cecil scratches under his nose with the end of a tiny screwdriver. "I fix one thing, and something else breaks. I get the feeling he doesn't want to come back or some such. I'll keep trying, but this might be the end of the poor egg man. Of course, I could revive him with a major rebuild, but that would take forever. I'd like to get back to working on the tunnels."

"Whatever you want to do," Nichelle says.

Cecil salutes us using his screwdriver, and we turn to the arched doorway with a column of carved goblin faces on either side. Of course, they only look carved. I'm sure in actuality the faces are made of plaster or cement.

We enter the Keep, and I don't know why, but I'm half-expecting to find a line of spartan cots where everyone sleeps. Instead, I'm inside a dining area with thick wooden tables and thick wooden chairs all clearly bolted to the floor. The tables and chairs surround a food kiosk in the center of the room. Winged rabbits perch on top of the refreshment booth, gazing down at us with kind-looking eyes, their mouths overly packed with fake french fries and hot dogs and pizza slices.

The room's empty, other than a man and woman sitting at one of the tables, dressed in matching, lavender tracksuits. They're singing some saccharine-sweet duet while tossing popcorn into a metal tankard on their table. We stand watching them for a few moments, but they don't turn our way. I may have seen them at the wedding, but I don't remember speaking to them.

"Hey," Nichelle says, and the two finally stop singing. "This is Corinna. The one I told you about. This is Evangeline and Cassian."

"Hi," I say. These are two more names I'll need to add to the list on my note app later.

"Welcome, welcome," Cassian says, lifting a hand and wriggling his fingers.

"We were hoping we'd run into you before tonight," Evangeline says. "Do you have any dietary restrictions we should know about?"

"I'm vegetarian," I say.

"I told you," Cassian says.

Evangeline tosses a piece of popcorn at him and manages to hit his shoulder. "You're not psychic," she says. "You're the opposite of psychic. Stop trying to make psychic happen."

Cassian tosses a piece of popcorn at her and misses by a mile. "You think you have me all figured out."

"I do. You have no intuition whatsoever."

"I was right about the vegetarianism."

"Half the people here are vegetarian."

Cassian throws another piece of popcorn, and he misses again.

"We'll have veggie burgers and veggie hot dogs," Evangeline says, looking at me again. "And veggies. I don't know if

Nichelle's told you, but tonight's pirate night and we're hosting. I hope you can make it. And I hope you like sea shanties."

"I can't say that I've heard many," I say. "Not since my pirate days at least."

Cassian laughs and Evangeline says, "You'll have to regale us with some tall tales of the sea. Topher usually dominates story hour, but his stories can be awfully morbid and bloody. I shouldn't assume that your stories aren't morbid and bloody, but I'm hoping for the best."

"I could tone down the gore a bit," I say.

"Thank Selanthian," she says. "Have fun on the grand tour. And Nichelle, make sure that you talk up pirate night. We need her there. As a pirate, or an ex-pirate, she'll add a sense of authenticity to the whole event."

"I'll do what I can," Nichelle says.

I have no idea who or what Selanthian is, but according to the cultist guidebook, bizarre words like that don't creep me out. Nope, not at all. Just keep smiling, Seraphina. We say our goodbyes, and then Nichelle leads me to the opposite side of the dining room where she presses a red button on the wall. A massive elevator door slowly opens and we step inside. What I notice, first and foremost, is the three-dimensional goblin head protruding from the faux-stone wall, wearing a burlap cap on his head.

As soon as the elevator door closes behind us, the goblin's eyes open and he says, "Where's it to be? Floor two? Floor three? You seem formidable, as far as humans go, but I doubt you're tough enough to press the skull and descend into the Underbelly. The Underbelly is not for the faint of heart. Where's it to be?"

Nichelle presses the button for the second floor.

"I knew it," the goblin says and cackles. "Maybe next time you will dare to descend into the world below. Next time." Then he closes his eyes.

Nichelle says, "The Underbelly's where the previous owner used to keep all the horror games. Zombie shooters and stuff like that. There's still a couple down there that the old owner never sold off."

The elevator opens on the second floor, and I glance at the goblin, but he doesn't say anything.

We step out into an open area scattered with dormant arcade games, pinball machines, an air hockey table, and a row of skee-ball lanes. As I'm searching the arcade for who-knows-what, I notice a marquee on one of the machines that reads *Goblintropolis USA*.

"There's a Goblintropolis game on every floor," Nichelle says. "Binkler had them specially made for the park, and I guess each one's a little different. You can plug them in and try them out, if you're interested."

"Are they fun?" I say.

"I don't know. I like air hockey. Topher's obsessed with the Goblintropolis game in the Underbelly, which means it's probably pretty gruesome."

"Ah."

We weave our way among the games and end up approaching three enormous claw machines all pressed together in a row.

"This is it," Nichelle says. "Our room, I mean."

"Oh great," I say. "I love the thought of sleeping in a claw machine on a pile of knockoff Bugs Bunnies."

Nichelle snorts and leads me around the claw machines, and I'm realizing now that someone's arranged these claw machines and racing games to form a makeshift room. We enter this little room-within-a-room by passing through a curtain of golden beads. Inside, I find two beds with soft ivory comforters, and two dressers, and a fluffy white rug that covers most of the floor. Sheets of linen cover the inner walls, embellished with pressed leaves. On Nichelle's side of the room, the dresser's topped with carved, painted candles as well as a tree sculpture made of twisted wire. A dozen or so necklaces hang from the branches.

"What do you think?" Nichelle says. "There are a couple other spaces available, if you'd like to check those out first."

"No," I say. "This is good. Of all the bedrooms hidden in an arcade I've ever stayed in, this is the nicest."

"Ha ha."

I roll my suitcase over to my new dresser, and when I look back over at Nichelle, she's sitting on the edge of her bed, wriggling her now bare feet in the fluffy rug.

She stares down at the rug and says, "I know you're trying to hide it, but I can tell you're a little freaked out." She looks up at me. "I want you to know that you don't have anything to be afraid of here. We're unconventional, and some of our spiritual processes can be somewhat challenging, but in the end we're all about creating better lives for ourselves. Like Ernie says, you're here to explore the labyrinth of your heart and find out what's at your center."

"Okay," I say. "Good to know."

"What else did I want to tell you?" She uses her toes to grip the fake fur at her feet and lift the rug slightly. "Oh. I'm sure you've noticed that at the retreat, we don't really carry around our phones. Our philosophy here is that the internet's chock-full of voices telling us what to think and what to want. Here, we want to quiet those voices as much as possible, so that we can hear our own thoughts. To be sure, you can use your phone whenever you feel like it, but if you could limit your usage to when you're alone, that would be awesome. That would help those of us trying to break the habit. I hope you don't mind."

"No," I say. "That's fine."

As far as the cultist guidebook goes, there's nothing weird

at all about disconnecting yourself from the rest of the world in this way. This doesn't faze Corinna at all.

"Awesome," Nichelle says. "Do you want to hang out here for a while, or should we continue on?"

"Let's keep going."

As I'm walking away from my new home away from home, I squeeze my over-the-shoulder purse to make sure that it didn't magically dematerialize. Yes, I still have my phone and my pepper spray.

When the elevator door closes, the goblin opens one eye and says, "Where's it to be? Floor three? Floor one? Most humans I've encountered are much too spineless to brave the horrors of the Underbelly, but I do detect a glimmer of gallantry in your eyes. Where's it to be?"

Nichelle uses her finger to unstick the closed eye of the goblin, so that now he has both eyes open.

"Which floor are we headed to?" I say.

"Back to one," she says.

I press the button for the ground floor, and the goblin shrieks with laughter. "I can't say your lack of courage surprises me. You humans are all alike. Maybe next time you will dare to descend into the world below, but for now, please enjoy the eateries at our food court. I recommend the goblin dog, which they assure me isn't made from real goblins."

We leave the Keep then, and we continue the grand tour. Nichelle shows me a laser tag arena that the Dredgers partially emptied out for an arts and crafts space. Murals of storm clouds and veins of gold lightning cover the walls and ceiling. Winged rabbits the size of human beings dangle from gossamer-thin wires that I can only see at certain angles. The rabbits look wide-eyed and fearful. I'm guessing all the foam rain clouds in the corner of the room were once scattered throughout the arena and used as obstacles and hiding spots.

Most of the Dredgers in this space are gathered at one massive table, some cutting up soda cans to look like moths or butterflies, others sanding the rough edges. There's already a pile of finished insects piled in the center of the table. I recognize Topher from the wedding, but the others I don't know yet. They all smile and greet me as if we're old friends.

"These are pretty."

"They're for the Revelries," Nichelle says. "That's a festival night coming up soon. The Selanight Revelries is pretty much an excuse to drink and crank up the dial of my merry-o-meter and maybe try something new. The night also holds a divine significance, but it's mostly about the partying."

"Sounds like fun." Corinna is extremely interested in all things Dredger, so says the guidebook. I need to ask more questions. "So what do the butterflies or moths represent?"

"Nothing really," Nichelle says. "Every year, we draw straws to see who gets to choose the theme, and Evangeline chose moths. She's loved them since she was a kid, and we try to honor our inner children during the Revelries."

"I see."

We move on from the moth station, and we approach a massive quilt hanging on one of the walls. The quilt features overlapping shapes that form the words *IN THE GLIM-MER OF SELANTHIAN*. Isn't that the word Evangeline mentioned earlier?

"What's that mean?" I say, nonchalantly, as if I'm asking about the soup of the day.

Nichelle glances at the quilt. "It's difficult to explain in a few words. But basically . . . Selanthian is the energy we're attempting to cultivate here in the park. It's a spirit of love and understanding and joy."

"Interesting."

Nichelle then shows me her dedicated worktable with all her paints and delicate-looking carving tools all lined up in neat rows. An unfinished candle depicts a small boy, sitting on what looks like an upside-down laundry basket, gesturing dynamically with his hands. His expression looks earnest and impassioned. I can imagine him speaking a mile a minute.

"I might have to start this one over from scratch," Nichelle says. "I'm not really doing him justice."

"What do you mean?" I say. "It's great. It really is."

Nichelle stares at the candle for a while and then says, "When we were kids, my brother would come into my room and dump my laundry on the floor and sit on the basket. His name was Steven. We'd talk for hours sometimes." With a fingertip, she repositions one of her carving tools that's slightly out of place. "I'd show him my weird drawings, and he'd describe all the video games he wanted to make one day. He'd tell me entire plots of movies that I wasn't allowed to see yet. I can't even remember half the things we talked about. When Steven moved out, I didn't think about the basket conversations for a long time. But then, when he was twenty or so, he came back for a visit. And that first night back, he came in my room and dumped out all my laundry, and we talked like we used to. That's when it really hit me how much I missed him. It hit me like a bus." She gently knocks on the table. "Alright, let's move on."

Nichelle mentioned before that she's lost loved ones, and judging by the phrase "his name was Steven," this is someone she lost. That's some top-notch detective work there, Seraphina. Before coming to the cult compound, I promised myself that deep down, I would remain guarded and detached. But I can feel my heart swelling a little in my chest. I remind myself that even if Nichelle seems genuine, she could be telling me the same story she tells every new recruit. This could be her way of bonding me to her and making me feel safe in her company. Who knows if any of this is even true?

The tour continues, and we pass through the Wolf King's

Dungeon, which they've converted into a gym, and we explore the nutrition center that was once Doctor Owl's Alchemy Lab. I can see why Eff would be so enamored by this place. She's always loved whimsical shit like this, and I guess so have I.

I meet Atticus, and Marisol, and Ocean, and Carly. I repeat their names in my head, the same way Nichelle repeated my impostor name. "Atticus Atticus Atticus Atticus Atticus Atticus." I store their faces and mannerisms and interests in a case file in my head. During the tour, Nichelle tells me a little bit about the energy work I'm going to begin tomorrow, and I try to act pleased. The cultist guidebook says that a day without energy work and other spiritual bullshit is a day wasted.

By the evening, I'm tired. I hardly slept last night, and I'm the sort of exhausted that you can feel in the center of your bones. But I need to show these people that Corinna's eager to be here. I need to create bonds. I can't waste my time sleeping.

And so I follow Nichelle across the rope bridge, over the Endless Lake, to the sailing ship that sits motionless in the center of this chemical-laced body of water. Despite the name, the Endless Lake isn't much greater in diameter than the sailing ship itself. All my new best buddies chat on the deck, eating and drinking, some of them wearing goblin masks or pirate hats or both. Most everyone's sitting on wicker armchairs and metal folding chairs that I recognize from the wedding. Glass parrots perch here and there on barrels and crates, their bodies lit up like phoenixes. My eyes are also drawn to a cheesecloth phantom floating at the helm, their willowy fingers gripping the handles of the wheel.

"Oh good," Evangeline says, as she speedwalks toward us. She's dressed in a laced-up striped shirt and tattered black pants. Her fake goatee's already peeling off her face. A fabric butterfly decorates the top of her blood-red headscarf. "You made it."

"I couldn't miss it," I say. "Nichelle convinced me that eating barbecue is an important part of the spiritual enlightenment process."

"Extremely vital," Nichelle says.

"What can I get for you?" Evangeline says. "We have veggie burgers, veggie hot dogs, corn, marinated veggie kabobs. I wouldn't be able to forgive myself if I didn't warn you, but Cassian's been coming up with his own recipes at the nutrition center and his veggie burgers tonight are best described as experimental. Once his batch of veggie burgers run out, he'll move on to cooking Atticus's batch. And Atticus definitely knows what he's doing. Should I get you both some kabobs for now?"

We agree that's for the best, and Evangeline speeds away toward the grilling area and returns with our paper plates. The two of us then join the rest of the group. At this point, almost everyone's listening to Topher, who's standing on a crate, a glass parrot illuminating him from below with kaleidoscopic light.

"He had no clue what he was doing there, man," Topher says. "The last thing he remembered was lying on his couch, watching a black-and-white movie about a plague. And then he found himself standing in the clearing where he buried her. He thought he must be dreaming. Then, all of a sudden, he started floating up, up, up." Topher lifts himself on his tippy toes and he loses his balance. Lucky for him, he manages to avoid falling off the crate. "He started floating up, up, up. He thought he must be flying, but when he looked down, he noticed his body was still standing there on the ground. He realized then what was happening. His neck was stretching, man. It was stretching like everything. His head kept rising, higher, higher, higher, and when he tried to scream, his voice sounded like a stranger's. His voice box was elongated. His neck grew faster, faster, and he was afraid that his head might lift all the way out of the atmosphere, where he'd suffocate. But his neck finally stopped, and when he looked down, he guessed his head was only a hundred feet or so in the air." The cultist glances around himself. "Yikes, where'd I put my drink?"

"Behind you," two people say, simultaneously.

Topher turns around and grabs his metal tankard and takes a generous gulp. Facing us again, he says, "He noticed then that his arms were elongating away from his torso, the same way his neck elongated. He could hardly feel his limbs at this point. He could really only feel a slight restless sensation traveling up his neck. As time passed, he realized that not only were his arms growing and stretching, so were his fingers. His fingers extended and split apart. Those bisected digits also extended and split apart. When he screamed again, he sounded even less like himself than before. He sounded like a high-pitched whistle." Topher puts two pinkies into his mouth and whistles louder than any human being has a right to. "He didn't know what to do, man. He knew for sure now that this wasn't a dream, because he still couldn't wake up. He tried to walk. He thought that if he could find his way back to civilization, some doctor might be able to reverse whatever was happening to him. But no matter how hard he tried, he couldn't move his legs. As you'd expect, he got thirsty as hell after a while. He constantly searched the sky for clouds, and he imagined himself opening his mouth and drinking the rain as it fell. But the sky remained clear. He also tried to will his feet to stretch into the ground like roots, so that he could search out some water there, but his feet wouldn't listen. So in the end, he just stood there, licking his lips and whistling as he tried to yell for help. Birds perched on his arms and fingers, but all the other animals stayed away. After a time, he died there in the same spot, right over the grave that he'd dug a year before. That's it."

The Dredgers applaud as Topher climbs off his tiny stage.

Several times today I've heard mention of Topher's obsession with blood and gore. The Dredgers seem slightly unnerved by him. Does Topher's fascination with violence mean that he's capable of hitting George with a car or pushing Eff into a quarry? I don't know. I love listening to true crime podcasts, but that doesn't mean I would hurt anybody. Nevertheless, I should probably put a star next to Topher's name in my notes.

After a while, Evangeline steps out in front of the crate, holding a large, metal spatula. "Does anyone else have a story?" she says, and then points the spatula at my face. "I'm looking at you, Captain Corinna. Any tales of mischievous mermaids or sassy sea monsters?"

I know I should get up there and perform for these people. I need them to like me.

"Next time," I say.

Evangeline doesn't argue. Maybe she can see the fatigue in my face.

Maintaining my Corinna facade is mentally exhausting. No matter what I keep telling myself, this isn't just another performance at a princess party. If I slip up and they find out who I really am, who knows what they'll do to me? This fear keeps hold of me like a leech.

"I'll go," Carly says, to my right. She sits on the crate and starts telling us about the summer she worked as a deodorant tester. I can hardly keep my eyes open, although that's only partially Carly's fault. Partway through the story, someone shouts, "Oh Jesus!"

I look over, and Marisol's standing by the railing at the edge of the deck, her left hand pressed against the side of her face.

"I saw a face in the fucking water," she says, to no one in particular.

A few people join her by the railing and lean over the edge.

"What kind of face was it?" Carly says, still sitting on the storytelling crate. I can detect a hint of irritation in her voice.

"I don't know," Marisol says. "It looked human. Human-ish. I was probably seeing things. It just fucking scared me is all." She laughs.

Behind her, Ernie inspects the water with his flashlight.

"It was probably nothing," Marisol says.

I'm sure she's right, but my anxiety right now is a winged rabbit shrieking in a thundercloud. I notice Cassian focusing all his attention on the grill, ignoring the water, ignoring Marisol. Does that mean anything?

"I see it," Ernie says, still shining his light at the water. "It's a dead possum."

"Oh thank Selanthian," Marisol says, and she laughs nervously again. "I'm sorry for freaking the fuck out. Sorry for interrupting your story, Carly."

"It's fine," Carly says.

Once Carly finishes her story, I leave the party early. Nichelle insists on walking me back to the Keep. After Topher's story and the whole face in the water situation, I'm a bit creeped out, and I'm grateful for Nichelle's company. But I shouldn't really feel too grateful, should I? Nichelle's sticking with me because I'm a new recruit. She wants to keep an eye on me. Maybe she's even walking me back to the Keep to make sure I won't sneak out of the park and escape.

We pass by the carnival booths, and I say, "Did you ever find out what happened to Sunglasses Cat?"

After a few moments of silence, Nichelle says, "He wrote us a letter. Did I not mention that?"

"No, you didn't."

"Yep. He ran off with some anthropomorphic spoon. It's just like that nursery rhyme. The cat ran away with the spoon."

"I think it's traditionally a dish. The dish ran away with the spoon."

"Oh yeah. Well, they're a pretty untraditional couple. They refuse to meet our societal expectations of who cats and spoons should run away with."

"Good for them. So how are they doing? Where are they living now?"

"They're on the moon. He says that they're doing well on an emotional level, but they're struggling financially."

"Is it because the moon is a desolate wasteland devoid of life?"

"No, the moon actually has a pretty healthy job market these days. But Sunglasses Cat doesn't have a work history to speak of, and Spoon's an aspiring stand-up comedian. Spoon's putting all his energy into that right now."

"That's tough."

At this point, we reach the entrance to the Keep.

Nichelle says, "I'm going to help clean up at the ship, but I'll see you later if you're still awake."

"No, I'll be out like a light by then," I say. "By the way, I hope you like snoring that sounds like a demon with asthma.

"That's my favorite kind of snoring. Did I not mention that earlier?"

We say goodnight and Nichelle walks away. I'm a little surprised by our whole cat and spoon conversation. Nichelle has definitely upped her absurdity to a new level. Did she pick up on the fact that I enjoy silly conversation like this, and she's trying to give me what I want? Or is this the Nichelle that naturally comes out when she's more comfortable with someone?

When the elevator door closes, the goblin says, "Where's it to be? Floor two? Floor three? You seem formidable, as far as—"

I press the second floor, and he shuts up for a second.

Then he says, "I knew it. Maybe next time you will dare to descend into the world below. Next time."

I make my way to my strange new bed, in my strange new room. I usually like to read a bit before going to sleep, but tonight I crawl under the covers and close my eyes. I need to rest up so that I can be alert for the big day tomorrow. Tomorrow, apparently, Ernie's going to dissect my soul.

EIGHT

By the time I wake up in the morning, Nichelle's already gone and her bed's made. The only evidence that she's been here at all is that the spoon pendant she was wearing yesterday is hanging on her tree sculpture. Eventually, I also find a note resting on my suitcase that reads: *Oops, I forgot to tell you yesterday, there's a door to the bathroom by the skee-balls. We only have a toilet and a shower. Sorry if you prefer baths.*

Minutes later, I lock myself in the bathroom and let the shower run while I make my call to the hospital. I'm not sure if the running water will actually prevent someone from listening in to my conversation, but spies do this in movies, so it's worth a try.

The doctor tells me what she always tells me. Eff still hasn't woken up.

Showered and dressed and somewhat mentally prepared for whatever the hell Ernie's planning for me today, I take the stairs down to the dining area and I find Nichelle writing notes on an extra-large sketch pad. A tiny cat sits on the medieval table, wearing rimless sunglasses and a neon windbreaker, a miniature stuffed version of our lost prize.

"Is that who I think it is?" I say.

"Yep," Nichelle says, tapping the cat's head with her orchid-print pen.

"Was he hit with a shrink ray?"

"Wow, how did you guess that?"

"Seriously though, where did you find this little replacement?"

"Replacement? I don't know what you mean. This is the same cat hit with a shrink ray."

I take a seat and say, "Hi cat. So it didn't work out with you and the spoon?"

"Oh no, Spoon's here too." Nichelle lifts her spoon from off her half-eaten plate of scrambled tofu and homestyle potatoes. "They both felt that moving a little closer to LA would help with Spoon's career."

"That's probably a good idea. The moon is a bit far from all the action."

After I eat, I stick the minuscule version of Sunglasses Cat in my purse, and we head out.

On the way to Ernie's analysis room, I remind myself that I'm supposed to be excited about today. I should smile. I should show them that there's absolutely nothing I want more than to spend an hour or whatever alone with a filthy-rich cult leader with a Peter Pan complex who wants to crack open my soul and see what's inside.

As we approach the fallen giant, Nichelle says, "Are you nervous? You've been a little quiet."

"Oh no," I say. "Just thinking."

"I was nervous before my analysis, but there's really nothing to it. You just answer some questions, and Ernie does the rest. And this process will do you so much good. I promise you that."

We walk around the head of the giant, and there's a wooden door on the back of his skull similar to the one at the entrance to the park. Someone's carved a spiral of intersecting shapes into the door.

I say, "I thought Ernie said there was no room in the head."

Nichelle grabs the doorknob shaped like a cluster of eye-balls. "I think he said there wasn't one when he was a kid. He had one made when he bought the park."

A scent like some combination of roses and wet dog invades my nose as soon as I step inside. Next to a shiny massage table, Ernie's sitting on a stool, dressed in a white button-down and khakis. He's reading a small book that looks like it's about to fall to pieces in his hands. A fountain gurgles in the corner of the room, consisting of a segment of petrified tree trunk, and a human-like fish balanced upright on top, water trickling from his puckering lips. Cheesy, ethereal spa music tinkles from white speakers. Slightly askew paintings on the wall depict waterfalls and giant sequoias and a semi-transparent fairy dancing on a sunflower. There's a fairy tale-looking, jewel-encrusted ax displayed next to the paintings, gripped by two iron hands protruding from the wall. Below the ax, there's also a crown made from woven reeds, decorated with acorns and small pine cones and golden flowers.

"Hello again," Ernie says, standing, and smiling. He holds out his book so that the cover's facing us, but I can't see a title. "Are you a fan?"

"The writing's too faded to read," Nichelle says.

All I can really make out on the cover is a woman's blurry face. The image makes her look as if she's moving her head back and forth too fast to be perceived clearly.

"Oh, right," Ernie says. "Never mind. It's not import-ant." He sets the book on an hourglass-shaped marble table, and then he ushers me toward the massage table. "Let's get started, shall we?"

"Do you want me to go?" Nichelle says. "Or should I stay?"

I can't tell if she's speaking to me or Ernie, but I say, "You can stay."

She sits on a velvet chair near the fish fountain, and I make my way onto the massage table.

"If you could lie on your back, that would be fantastic. Cool. Thank you. Now relax your breathing. In. Out. In. Out. Perfect." He holds his hands in the air above my torso, twitching his fingers sporadically as if he's playing an invisible instrument. "In order to progress with the energy analysis, I need you to grant me access to your spiritual depths. This, however, is easier said than done. What I need from you is to recall a moment in time when you felt completely safe, or at least as close to completely safe as you've ever felt. I'm sure you're thinking, 'what the hell is this guy on about,' and I don't blame you." He laughs. "None of this will make much sense to you at first, but believe me when I say the process works." He wiggles his fingers even more energetically than before. "Opening up a comforting memory to me will create a bond between us that will allow me deeper into your psyche. I know that I'm still a stranger to you, and that you don't exactly trust me yet. But I ask you to take this leap of faith, for your own sake."

Of course, I don't know what the fuck he's talking about, but I say, "Okay."

"Cool." He closes his eyes and continues moving his fingers. "Now try to conjure up your memory of safety as vividly as possible. Tell me every detail that pops into your mind. Every image, every feeling will strengthen the bond between us."

"Okay," I say, and I clear my throat. "I was bullied in middle school. Lunch was hell until my English teacher Mrs. Hill let me and a few other kids stay in her room. We—"

"I'm afraid I have to stop you," Ernie says. "This feels false to me."

Can he actually tell that I'm lying?

He gradually lowers his arms to his side, as if he's moving

in slow motion. He opens his eyes. He says, "What you're describing is a temporary respite from suffering. That's not the same as feeling perfectly safe, and I'm afraid a memory of relief or escape is not going to cut it here. I need you to find a moment where you didn't have a care in the world. This is easier said than done, I know, but I'm sure you can find me something."

"Okay."

I take another deep breath. I try to come up with a convincing lie, but I can't think. I need to say something. Maybe I can mix some lies with the truth, like in one of the semi-bullshit stories I tell Eff.

"I'm in the backseat of my mom's Ford Taurus," I say. "It's late at night, and I'm sleepy, and my mom's driving me home. Classic rock's playing on the radio with the volume lowered almost to the point where I can't hear it. My mom has this way of driving where she presses her right wrist against the wheel and snaps her fingers. She snaps to the music."

Of course, in reality, I never felt safe with my mother. After my dad passed away, she became a religious fanatic who treated me like a sinful annoyance, but even before that, she was never pleasant to be around.

Ernie's closing his eyes again and wriggling his fingers.

I can hear Nichelle snoring softly in the corner.

For some reason, I'm feeling slightly light-headed. That scent of roses and wet dog smells more potent than ever, but maybe I'm only imagining that.

"I take off my seatbelt and I lie down, stretched out across the back seat. I kick off my shoes. I press my feet against the cold window. My mom would tell me to sit up and buckle up if she noticed what I was doing, but she doesn't. I have no concept at this age of how dangerous cars can be. I feel completely invincible because my mom's at the wheel."

This is, in truth, a memory of my dad driving me around. I

don't feel as relaxed as my childhood self stretched out across the back seat, but I feel calm. Too calm. I shouldn't let my guard down so much.

"Cool," Ernie says, opening his eyes again. "That's enough. You can sit up."

I do what he says.

He then strolls over to the marble table and spends the next thirty seconds or so scribbling in a small notebook. Once he's finished, he rips out the paper. He hands me a drawing of various overlapping circles and irregular polygons.

"I know this doesn't look like much," he says, and he takes a seat on the stool. "But this is your passkey. This passkey is what will allow you to pierce through the more superficial layers of your psyche and access your core. And if you're thinking, 'what kind of gobbledygook is this guy talking about,' I don't blame you. This whole key business sounded like gobbledygook to me too, at first." He stands again, despite the fact that he just sat down. "We could sit here together for the next hour or two, and I could elucidate on the finer points of energy work, but at the end of my lecture, you still wouldn't truly understand anything. Words, in and of themselves, aren't enough to express truth when it comes to these kinds of spiritual matters. In order to understand how your passkey can help you explore the labyrinth of your heart, you need to use your passkey. Nichelle will show you how to do that. She's a better teacher than I'll ever be." He turns to her. "Nichelle. Nichelle."

She opens her eyes.

"Corinna's ready for the next step," Ernie says, and he grabs his ancient-looking book from the table. The woman on the cover stares at me with ill-defined, cerulean eyes. "I'll see you both later."

Outside of the giant's head, Nichelle says, "I'm sorry I fell asleep back there. It's that music. It always gets me."

"Don't worry about it," I say.

Nichelle studies my face, and I try to make my smile look as natural as possible.

"I know it's all pretty confusing," Nichelle says. "But everything Ernie says will make perfect sense to you eventually. I promise you that."

Yes, that's exactly what I want, Nichelle. There's nothing in the world I want more than to be of one mind with a cultist who spends his days wiggling his fingers above people's stomachs in the head of a giant. Wouldn't that be a beautiful thing?

After lunch, Nichelle laminates my mystical passkey in the laser tag arena, and she traces me another copy, in case I lose the original.

"Thanks," I say, smiling, and stuffing both pieces of laminated trash into my purse.

We move on to the Haunted Mirror Maze for my first session.

As we approach the building, my reflection stares at me, growing bigger and bigger with every step. This time, my doppelganger's more head than body. I can't read her expression, because her eyes and nose and mouth are all crammed together in the center of her face.

Nichelle stops us a few yards from the front entrance, and she speaks in a hushed tone. She says, "A bunch of us come here every day after lunch, although the energy center's always open, day or night. For sure, you can meditate using your passkey anywhere at any time, but it's nice to have a dedicated area where people aren't constantly talking. I'm sure you've noticed that many of the Dredgers can be a tad boisterous."

"I've noticed," I say.

"What happens now is, I'll show you your spot inside, and you'll concentrate on your symbol. Some people, like Cecil, can mentally visualize his symbol with his eyes closed, but it's perfectly fine to look at your paper." She retrieves a small card from her bag, illustrated with her own unique throng of geometric shapes, and bordered with an intricately painted wreath of milkweed flowers. "I always look at my paper. What happens when you're focusing on your symbol varies quite a lot from person to person, or even from session to session. I used to visualize myself in a lighthouse. Nowadays, I wander an old Victorian home." She takes a deep breath. "It's pretty much chock-full of secret passageways and hidden rooms. When I find a new room, I throw open the curtains. I light candles. I pull dusty sheets of fabric off the furniture. And as I bring light and life back to these chambers, I'm uncovering my authentic self. And there's more to all this than self-discovery. My rooms not only show me who I am, they act as beacons. They let the universe know that I'm ready to experience joy. That's the goal, anyway. We're all working to cultivate a reality of authentic merriment, or Selanthian." She carefully places her card back into her bag. "Do you have any questions for me before we go in?"

"No," I say. "I'm good."

Because what could I possibly ask? Nichelle simply wants me to wander around a lighthouse or an old Victorian home in my mind, light candles, and create magical beacons to attract Selanthian. That all makes perfect sense.

What was once a maze, the Haunted Mirror Maze now consists of numerous, polygonal cubicles formed from inwardly facing mirrors. When Nichelle leads me into a free cubicle, my reflections move around me, duplicated into infinity. The effect's more than a little jarring, and I almost trip on nothing at all.

After regaining my composure, I unroll the yoga mat that I picked out at the Wolf King's Dungeon. Nichelle's watching me, smiling, so I sit down and take the laminated sheet out of my purse. I carefully place the paper right in front of me on the mat.

"Good luck," Nichelle mouths at me, and leaves me alone with my many reflections.

I reposition my legs and roll my head around and try to get comfortable. No one so much as hinted to me how long one of these sessions traditionally lasts, so I have no idea how long I should sit here like this. What if the Dredgers wander their inner labyrinths for three hours at a time, and then I stroll out of here in fifteen minutes? They might assume I'm not here for the right reasons.

The thought also creeps into my head that they could be watching me with a hidden camera. Nichelle has hardly left my side since I arrived at the park. Maybe they want to make sure that I am who I'm pretending to be.

Last year, the mother of a birthday girl called me up to notify me with pride in her voice that she had hidden cameras all over her yard. She said that when she reviewed the footage of the party, she noticed that I was on my phone, hiding behind a tree, while the birthday cake was being served. She said I didn't do my job. She demanded a retroactive discount. Of course, she could have told customer service about all this, but she wanted to speak with me personally. That's how angry she was.

The Dredgers could definitely be watching me.

For a while, I stare at my key, and as expected, nothing happens. I don't travel to a lighthouse or a labyrinth or a Victorian mansion full of secret passageways.

Somewhere in the Haunted Mirror Maze nearby, a woman roars with laughter. I picture her sitting on her yoga mat, alone in her cubicle, laughing her head off while gazing at Ernie's magical doodles.

I breathe deeply, pretending that I'm transcending the physical realm, and I can smell the same aroma of roses and dog that I detected in the Ernie's analysis room. Maybe this is some sort of incense? But I don't remember seeing any incense in the giant's head. What if this smell is actually Ernie's cologne? What if I'm sitting next to a one-way mirror and Ernie's standing on the other side right now, staring at me?

This is why I hate meditation. Every time Eff convinced me to meditate with her, I tried to clear my head, but my consciousness simply scurried toward the darker corners of my imagination. There's nothing I enjoy more than freaking myself out, I guess.

I wonder if this is the cubicle where Eff focused on her own key and rediscovered her so-called psychic powers. Did she believe honing those powers would somehow help her achieve authentic merriment? I can see her sitting here, dressed in galaxy-print leggings and a tank with *INNER PEAS* printed on the front, right above an image of anthropomorphic peas in a yoga class. She's biting her upper lip with concentration. Images flash in her mind of Aunt Gloria's peonies and Dad's campfires and shards of glass in George's face.

I think about the summers after Dad died, when we stayed in Aunt Gloria's tiny apartment. I remember Aunt Gloria saying, "Someone's going to call us," and sometimes we would get a call shortly after. Once, Eff said, "Auntie, you're going to see an owl today," and when Aunt Gloria returned from her errands, she grinned and said, "Saw a barn owl." Once, late at night, I asked Eff if she truly believed we had powers, and she said it didn't matter if we did or not. Our powers didn't help us to save Dad, so they were useless anyway.

The woman nearby guffaws again, and this time her booming laughter's followed by spurts of nervous giggles. I wonder what she's seeing in her lighthouse or her labyrinth. I almost wish I could transport myself to some inner realm, because at least that would be a change of scenery. I'm tired of these polygons, and the incessant giggles, and the smell of wet dog. The worst part about all this isn't so much that I'm feeling miserable. It's the knowledge that I'll need to come back here for more sessions. Fuck this. I hate meditation.

I roll my head again and stretch my arms over my head.

Well, I might as well make the best of my time. I spend the next long while plotting and scheming and coming up with little monologues that might come in handy when dealing with the Dredgers.

Eventually, I decide that enough's enough. Certainly I've been sitting here for at least an hour. My internal clock is usually fairly dependable, but I'm honestly not sure how much time has passed.

I head out of the Haunted Mirror Maze, and I half-expect Nichelle to be sitting near the front entrance, waiting for me. But I don't see anyone except for my doppelganger in an exterior mirror. Her head's rounder than mine, and her eyes are much larger. She looks more like Eff than myself. She looks sad as hell.

After a moment, I walk away from her and for the fiftieth time today, an intelligent little voice in my head tells me to escape the park while I still can. I don't belong here. I belong in my shitty apartment on the ugliest, comfiest couch in the world, with Heracles purring on my lap. I belong in Eff's hospital room.

In a couple minutes, I'm back in the Keep, smiling my head off, telling Nichelle and Cassian and Evangeline that I wandered a moonlit forest of ponderosa pines and incense cedars and white firs. I tell them that I strolled through overgrown trails, brushing my fingertips against leaves and branches. I tell them that here and there I discovered ancient, wooden boxes nestled in the forest floor. I tell them that inside the boxes, I found objects from my past, and objects that I didn't recognize.

I'm not completely confident in all the bullshit I'm spouting, but thankfully, they swallow up my lies like hungry baby birds.

Once I'm in bed, I finally let myself relax. Somehow, I managed to navigate the absurdities and exceedingly tedious trials of today without letting my Corinna persona slip. Maybe I can actually do this. The labyrinth of my heart isn't swirling with authentic merriment, whatever the fuck that means, but I'm feeling a bit hopeful. Right now I'll take what I can get.

NINE

Three days creep by. Every morning, I lock myself in the bathroom and call the hospital, and the news is always the same. Eff still won't wake up. I feel horrible for not visiting her for so long, but the thought of stepping back into that hospital room saturates my whole body with dread, or some gnawing, rotting feeling worse than dread. What's the point of going back to the hospital, anyway? When I talk to Eff, I doubt she can hear me. At least here in the park, I might do some good. I might end up bringing her some justice.

Every day after lunch, I join the rest of the Dredgers in the Haunted Mirror Maze, and I stare at my shapes, and I wander the park in my head. I strike up conversations with different Dredgers and imagine how these conversations might play out. When I'm done with my meditations, I wander the park for real. I try to make friends. I want these people to trust me.

It's frustrating, but I still haven't heard anyone mention Eff or her so-called accident at the quarry. Maybe the Dredgers don't want to frighten me off by talking about something so horrible? I don't know. I need to figure out a way to broach the subject with them in a natural way. I'm guessing "hey, so has anyone here ever fallen into a pit" probably won't work.

For two nights in a row, shapes haunt my dreams and nightmares. In one, I'm having a picnic, and I notice triangles written on the clouds. When I turn to Alvin to tell him about the clouds, I notice polygon-shaped hives all over his forehead. Back in my apartment, I open my window and hundreds of circles fly in from outside and swarm my face. When I scream, they funnel into my throat. I guess this all means I should stop spending so much time in the Haunted Mirror Maze, gazing at my shapes. Maybe I could stare at the empty space next to my passkey.

At the end of that third night, I'm sitting in a wicker chair, with Cecil on my left and an empty chair on my right. By now, everyone seems to know that Nichelle and I like to sit together at meals, so no one takes that spot beside me.

As I'm eating, I notice that the once-motionless phantom at the helm now turns the wheel left and right, again and again, guiding the ship nowhere. Their body radiates a soft, minty green light. Every day that I'm here, more bits and pieces of the park come to life. You never know what's going to open its eyes or speak to you.

"Is this your doing?" I say, motioning toward the phantom.

"Nah," Cecil says, and he stabs a roasted cherry tomato with his pocketknife. "I'm thinking Ocean fixed that one."

"Ah."

And this concludes yet another riveting tête-à-tête between me and Cecil. The two of us should start a vaudeville act.

Beyond Cecil, Marisol's standing at the edge of the deck, gazing out at a dark section of the park. Marisol's a big fan of standing around and gazing at nothing.

Atticus passes by her, saying, "See any more faces out there?"

"Shut up," Marisol says, not playfully in the least.

Once Atticus is gone, I consider walking over and speaking with Marisol. I haven't spent much time with her yet. I still need to figure out if she's the sort of person who would throw someone to their near-death.

Right after I stand up, Nichelle takes her traditional seat to my right.

"You made it," I say, and I sit again.

"Don't give me that I-told-you-so look," she says.

"I'm not. It's just that I told you that you needed a break, and now you're here taking a break. It's just interesting that I was right all along."

"Ha."

Nichelle turns away from me and starts reapplying her lipstick.

I haven't seen as much of Nichelle the last few days as I did when I first arrived. She disappears for hours at a time to work on her candles or whatever other projects she has going on. I often catch her sitting alone on an artificial grass tuffet, drawing bizarre diagrams and composing dense, esoteric paragraphs that I sneak peeks at sometimes. I've spotted mentions of awareness strata and incorporeal magnetism and other such gibberish. Maybe she's writing a book about Ernie's teachings?

Nichelle puts her lipstick away and says, "Is there any food left?"

"Sorry," I say. "I had a light lunch, so I ended up eating everything."

"Really. You even ate all the chicken? You're not a vegetarian anymore?"

"Yeah, I ate all the meat. I even ate the bones."

Nichelle leaves her bag on her chair and heads off toward the twin grills at the back of the ship. While she's gone, I busy myself gazing out into the darkness, Marisol-style.

I'm still gazing and rehearsing some lines in my head when Nichelle returns with an impressive heap of food on her plate.

"Don't judge," she says. "I'm hungry for a mountain of food, and I'm going to eat a mountain of food."

"No judgment," I say. "I'm just upset that Atticus and

Ocean hid some food stores from me. I told them to feed me everything on board. They'll pay for their insubordination."

At this point, Atticus walks out in front of the performance crate, wearing a *KICK THE COOK* apron.

"Okay," he says. "We've reached that moment of the night we've all been waiting for. Or possibly dreading. Story hour time. Who's first?"

I lick the potato salad off my spoon and hold the utensil out in front of me. "Are you sure you want to go up there?" I say. "This is a tough crowd."

"I think he'll be fine," Nichelle says. "I heard him practicing his set the other night. It's really funny. He has a great bit about his grandpa ladle."

"Okay. Good luck."

I toss the spoon at the performance crate, barely missing Topher as he passes in front of me.

"Yikes," Topher says. "Flying spoons."

"Sorry," I say.

Nichelle and I watch Spoon silently for a few seconds.

"Oh god," Nichelle says. "He's choking."

"Spoon, you can do this," I say. "Just say something."

At this point, Topher climbs up onto the crate and knocks Spoon off in the process.

Nichelle whispers, "This isn't going to do anything for Spoon's self-confidence."

I half-listen to Topher's story about a grad student who's hired as a playmate for a gray-haired hedge fund manager. The grad student doesn't know what to expect, because the ad for the job doesn't go into great detail. When he finally goes to the penthouse, he finds the manager dressed up like a baby. The two of them play with blocks. The student feeds the manager pureed carrots that the manager made that morning. I miss part of the story here, because I'm rehearsing parts of my own tale in my head. I need to express some vulnerability. I need to touch hearts.

Eventually, I focus on Topher's story again.

The manager demands that the student play the Box Game with him. The student says that he doesn't know how to play the game, and the manager throws a temper tantrum. He screams at the top of his lungs. He shatters his unwashed blender on the floor. After the tantrum, the manager uses his brute strength to squeeze the student into a box of thick glass, breaking many of the student's bones and rupturing his flesh. Topher mimes this brutal act in the empty space in front of him. Once the manager finishes, he places the glass box on a display shelf where he keeps all his favorite stuffed boxes.

The Dredgers applaud, halfheartedly for the most part.

"Wasn't that a delight," Atticus says. "So who's our next jabberer of the evening?"

I stand, and on my way to the performance area, I pick up poor Spoon. Then I hop up on the crate so that I can sit at the edge with the glass parrot beside me. This crate's so tall, my legs don't even touch the floor.

Topher lets loose one of his ear-splitting whistles, and Ernie gives me a thumbs-up, and Nichelle watches me attentively while ignoring her mountain of food. She looks so pretty tonight, bathed in moonlight.

I clear my throat, and I look past the crowd at the darkness beyond. I don't particularly like looking at faces when I'm performing, unless they're children, or unless they're Eff. Whenever she helped me read lines to prepare for an audition, or whenever I told her one of my semi-bullshit stories, she never made me feel self-conscious. "Like I'm sure many of you already know, I used to be a pirate, sailing the seven seas, stealing spices and other precious cargo, destroying armadas for inbred queens. It's satisfying work if you can get it. I have a million stories, but I should probably tell you about this thing that happened to me about five years ago." I tap Spoon's head against the edge of the crate. "I'll spare you the mundane details, but through no fault of my own, I ended up trapped on a desert island in the middle of the Bermuda Triangle. I was without a ship, without a crew, without my trusty parrot Mr. Parsnip." I balance Spoon on my shoulder. "Of course, I tried to make the best of things. I constructed a glamp-worthy shelter. I tried creating a radio out of coconuts but it's not as easy as it sounds. I also constructed a friend named Pillson out of an old Aspirin that I had in my purse. I ended up swallowing him, but that's a tragic tale for another day." Spoon falls off my shoulder and I somehow manage to catch him despite my infamously horrible reflexes. "One day, I was digging for measly little clams on the beach when a man popped out of the water nearby. He had long, platinum-blond hair and a wide, crooked smile. He cut right to the chase, informing me that he was a merman prince and that he wanted to invite me to his undersea kingdom for a visit. Of course, as a seasoned pirate, I didn't trust him yet. I've heard stories of mermen saving people's lives, but I've also heard of stories where they devour people's flesh and make crowns from their bones." I tap Spoon against my knee, trying to find that spot that would make my leg jump a little. I sometimes act silly when I'm nervous, but this isn't a silly story. I need to stop. "I told the merman that I didn't have any scuba gear on me, and that I couldn't exactly hold my breath long enough to take a tour of a castle. He laughed and said he had special powers that would allow me to breathe underwater and protect me from decompression sickness. He said that as long as I was stuck there on the island away from my people, I might as well enjoy myself. I told him I'd think about it."

I glance over at Topher to make sure he's listening to me. He is.

"The next day, I went out to collect more minuscule clams, and the merman surfaced again. He asked me if I was ready to join him yet, and I told him I was still thinking. He laughed and said that humans were certainly as distrustful as he'd heard. He said that since I wouldn't come to his kingdom, he would bring the wonders of his kingdom to me. So while I dug for clams, he described his world for me. He told me about his castle, made from hundreds of species. He ate dinner at a table of bright orange coral. Tapestries of heroes, both real and mythical, decorated the walls, made from woven sea grasses. The merman went on and on, and the next time I scavenged for clams, he continued his descriptions. He said that he spent much of his time in his library, writing letters on flattened kelp leaves using a pinkish-purple sea pen. He described his masquerade balls, where everyone wrapped themselves in jellyfish-skin robes and wore masks made from sea glass and fish bones and abalone shells. On their heads, they also wore antler-like coral coated with bioluminescent algae."

A plate or a glass shatters on the deck, causing me to jump a little.

Marisol says, "Sorry."

I continue, "At night, I imagined myself in his kingdom. I was tired of my shitty shelter. I was tired of eating clams and coconuts every fucking day. Eventually I decided that enough was enough, so I told the merman that I was ready, and I jumped into the water. He immediately wrapped his arms around me and pulled me into the sea. He didn't use any special powers to help me breathe. I struggled to free myself as he dragged me deeper and deeper into the ocean. I could see now that he wasn't a merman at all. He had a long, slimy body like an eel that stretched into the darkness below. I looked at his face, and he smirked at me, laughing with his bulbous eyes. I punched him and kicked him in slow motion. My lungs burned like hell. After an eternity of struggling, I managed to poke him in his eye, and he released me. He pressed his hands against his face. As he screamed, thousands of tiny, phosphorescent bubbles spewed from his mouth. I only looked at him for a second before kicking myself back to the surface. I was positive that at any moment he would grab me again. At one point I felt him wrap his fingers around my ankle, and I yelled, releasing most of my air. But when I looked down, the culprit turned out to be nothing but kelp. I needed air. My lungs felt like they were bursting apart inside me. I was still sure the eel man would catch me. Somehow, I managed to break the surface and breathe again. I swam toward the beach. I gave it everything I had, knowing that I probably wouldn't survive. But at least I'd know that I tried. And, as you're probably guessing since I'm talking to you right now, I reached the beach. I crawled across the warm sand, because I didn't have the strength to stand yet. After a few moments, I felt myself being pulled back toward the ocean. I dug my hands into the sand, trying to anchor myself. When I looked back, I spotted the eel man smirking and pulling the strand of kelp that was still wrapped around my ankle. With every passing moment, he was yanking me closer and closer to the water."

I thought I might force myself to cry a little during my performance, but I can feel real tears stinging my eyes. I thought the fantastical nature of the story would allow me some emotional detachment. Nevertheless, the woman and the merman remind me too much of Eff and George. I can see Eff's face that night she escaped to my apartment. I can hear her voice.

I continue, "My hands were shaking with fear and exhaustion, and I fumbled with the kelp around my ankle. The seaweed felt strong like rope. He continued to pull, and soon a wave crashed over me. I was back under the water. I was sure

I was going to die this time. And then, suddenly, I managed to free myself from the kelp. With a surge of energy, I swam and then crawled and then raced away from the water. I collapsed after a bit, and I sat on the sand, catching my breath. I kept my eye on the eel man the whole time I sat there, to make sure he wouldn't try anything else. And as I watched him, he towered above the waves, looking at me, wheezing with laughter. The end."

The Dredgers clap for me, and I wipe away a tear. I return to my seat, feeling staticky currents of energy in my arms and legs, the way I often do after a performance.

"That was great," Nichelle says, giving me one of those heartfelt smiles of hers that show up mostly in her eyes.

Once the ill-named story hour is over two hours later, I mingle and drink and dance. Late in the evening, I make my way over to Topher. I tell him that I'm in dire need of an arcade game partner and that I hear he's the guy to ask. His face lights up and he says, "Yeah, man."

And so, the next day, I find myself side-by-side with Topher, facing the floor two version of *Goblintropolis USA the Arcade Game*. From his jacket pocket, Topher removes a bulging coin purse with a dissected eyeball embroidered on the front. He dumps a small mountain of quarters on the control panel.

We play.

We're both goblins, and we start out riding winged bunnies over a range of jagged, purple mountains. We move around the screen, avoiding gusts of neon wind and hot air balloons made from animal furs. I'm doing okay until the fanged owls and the badgeresque creatures show up. The owls shoot us with barbed feathers, and the pointy-eared badgers chomp at us as they glide around wearing wingsuits. When I manage to hit an enemy with my tiny yellow hammer, they seem entirely unfazed.

I don't know how Topher can even play with all that hair covering his eyes, but I suppose he can see somehow. He's hardly dying at all.

A badger bites the head off my rabbit, and I plummet to certain doom, again.

"I'm sorry I keep dying," I say. "I'm using up all your coins."

"Oh no worries, man," he says. "When we're done, I'll just open up the machine and get them all back."

After a while, the owls and the badgers vanish, and we enter a fierce, 16-bit storm. This is when the Wolf King appears. He's enormous. He's strapped in some old-timey-looking flying contraption with dozens of undulating propellers.

Topher says, "This part's tough. If you position yourself under the lightning bolts and press the red button right when you're hit, you can swallow the electricity. Then you can spit out a nice energy blast at the wolf."

The Wolf King fills more and more of the screen until Topher's goblin hits him with a neon-green bolt. Then the wolf retreats slightly.

We hit him again and again, and I say, "How many more times until he blows up?"

"Oh, the Wolf King can't die," Topher says. "We can only slow him down."

I press the red button at the wrong moment, so the lightning bolt permeates my body and my hair bursts into green flames.

"I enjoyed your story last night," I say. "Really twisted. In a good way."

"Thanks," Topher says. "I really liked yours too."

The Wolf King slices my head off with a fancy-looking sword and I say, "I almost didn't tell that story. It can be difficult to talk about the eel man."

Topher laughs and then glances at me. "Oh, you're serious? Sorry."

"Yeah," I say. "The eel man's based on an actual guy. Loosely based." The Wolf King shoots a cannon at my trusty cottontail and blows her to pieces. "In reality, he wasn't actually an eel, at least not in the biological sense. He was likable at first, and he spoke with a sort of vividness that drew me in. He was good at describing the life he wanted us to build together." I think about Eff and the night in my apartment when she told me everything. The Wolf King roars. "For a few months, he managed to hide his true sadistic self from me, but eventually he showed me who he was, and he pulled me into the sea."

Topher looks over at me and lets his goblin die. "I'm sorry, man," he says. "That's rough. I'm so sorry that happened to you."

"Thanks," I say.

I appreciate Topher's kindness here, but of course "I'm so sorry" isn't what I want to hear. What I want is for Topher to grin and say, "He sounds like a guy who's in need of a good leg-breaking." Or, "I fucking hate guys like that. They all should be tossed into wells and left to rot."

I guess I should mentally cross Topher off my suspect list. He might be the Dredger most obsessed with violence and gore, but I can't imagine him actually harming anyone.

I sigh. Well, I'll just have to keep searching. Someone deserves to pay for what they did to Eff.

Topher and I trek through level after level of the game, and we end up in a forest populated by diaphanous phantoms. When the spirits possess our bodies, they force us to attack each other. They make us laugh.

Finally, we reach a gigantic, pea-soup-colored tree with ocher eyes and prismatic teeth and twitching hands.

"Be careful here, man," Topher says. "If the tree gets you, you're not just dead, you're dead-dead. Your soul's absorbed by the tree. It's game over and you can't continue, even if you put in another coin."

We fight the tree, throwing pebbles and mushrooms and twigs.

I give it everything I've got, but after half a minute, the tree grabs me with a cadaverous hand.

"Oh fuck," Topher says.

The tree pulls me close, and swallows me whole, and I'm gone.

TEN

I'm sitting cross-legged in the Haunted Mirror Maze when I realize that I can't move. I don't know what's wrong with me. I'm staring at my passkey, and I can't even move my eyes. The stench of flowers and wet dog intensifies with each passing moment. Maybe I've meditated for so long that my whole body's gone numb? Or maybe what I'm smelling is some sort of gas?

After who-knows-how-long, I manage to break free of whatever's holding me, I turn my attention away from the passkey. It only takes me a moment to realize that I'm trapped in here. Where there was once an opening in my cubicles, there's now another inwardly facing mirror.

Is this some sort of test? What do the Dredgers expect me to do here?

I stand and my reflections take a few seconds to follow my lead. I raise my hand. Seconds later, my reflections do the same.

Suddenly, my reflections change. There's a Seraphina with a bulbous head. There's a Seraphina with leathery skin stretched taut over the jagged bones of her face. There's a Seraphina with massive tusks stabbing through the roof her mouth and jutting from the top of her head.

I push at the mirror that's blocking my exit, and a

Seraphina pushes back at me with gooey eyes that trickle down her cheeks like tears. The mirror won't even budge.

"Nichelle?" I say. "Topher? Evangeline?"

If I could break out of here, I'm sure one of them could explain to me what's going on. I know there's probably someone dangerous living at the park, but most of the Dredgers seem as kind as Eff. I'm sure most of them want to help me.

I turn from the Seraphina with the melting eyes and I run as fast as I can, hopping over the yoga mat in the center of the cubicle. I slam my body against a random mirror. Another Seraphina crashes into me, wires and tubes sprouting from every orifice of her face.

I'm positive I left my phone on silent, but I hear the device tinkling from my purse on the floor. I answer the call.

Alvin appears on the screen, looking uncharacteristically grim.

"What's wrong?" I say. "Is it Eff?"

My reflections open their mouths, screaming in silence around me.

"Eff's not the one I'm worried about," Alvin says.

"What do you mean?" I say.

"You're dead."

My reflections continue to scream, and Alvin's mouth opens wider and wider until I hear a crack.

That's when I wake up in a cold sweat.

After breakfast, in reality, I make my way to the giant's head, because apparently Ernie's summoned me for a spiritual checkup.

Before long, I'm lying on my back on the black massage table and Ernie's twitching his fingers in the air above my face. I can see flecks of grime or paint under his fingernails.

"Take some deep breaths for me," he says. "In. Out. In. Out. Perfect. Thank you." He stops moving his fingers, and he keeps his hands curled like claws above me. "You're making impressive progress, Corinna. You've lit more internal beacons in a few days than others ignite in weeks or months. You seem naturally attuned to mystical arts. Now let me ask you a question." He lowers his hands to his sides. "Do you ever smell anything bizarre when you're in close proximity to your passcode?"

"Yeah," I say.

"And is this a strong scent, or can you barely perceive it?"

"Sometimes it's strong."

"I thought so."

Ernie turns away and sits on his stool, and I sit up, feeling a little light-headed.

"Nichelle could probably explain this better," he says, picking up the old book from off the marble table beside him. "She has a way of bringing clarity to the inexplicable. But I'll do my best." He rubs his thumb against the cover of the book. "Phantom smells and phantom images are a common occurrence here, because in a sense, the park is existing in two realities simultaneously. There's the world we're used to, and there's the realm of Selanthian energies. What you're smelling, when you're close to the Selanthian symbols, are those energies. The fact that they smell so potent to you is a testament to the strength of your extrasensory perceptions. Most people can't smell Selanthian at all."

I can see how lines like this would work on Eff. She eats up bullshit like this.

Ernie looks so smug sitting there, stroking his creepy old book, as if he has me eating from the palm of his hand. I'm sure he makes a habit of spraying this room with some pungent musk before I come in, to set me up for this little speech of his. He wants me to feel special.

He continues, "I called you here merely to verify what I already sensed was true. You're ready for the initiation." He holds the book against his chest, and I can see the woman's blurred face through his fingers. "I'm sure you're thinking 'an initiation sounds more appropriate for a frat house than a spiritual retreat.' But I assure you the ritual will be nothing but beneficial for your own wellbeing. To initiate you, your core will be saturated with Selanthian energies, which will bond you to us and to our realm, both symbolically and spiritually. You won't be harmed in any way. If this sounds agreeable to you, I'll begin the preparations, and we can hold the initiation in a couple of days. What do you think?"

Taking part in some weird Dredger ritual isn't exactly my idea of a good time, but I know I need to do this. Maybe if I'm truly one of them, they'll trust me enough to talk about Eff in my presence.

"That sounds good," I say.

Ernie sets the old book on his lap and picks up a small tape recorder from off the marble table. "Before we finish for the day, I'd like you to leave me with two or three questions you're hoping to answer through your work here at the retreat. Through my own processes, I'll imbue the questions with Selanthian energies. This will aid in the preparations for your initiation. Does that sound agreeable to you?"

Sure, Ernie. Whatever floats your metaphysical boat, buddy.

"Yeah," I say. "That sounds great."

He presses a red button on the recorder and gazes at me expectantly and says, "Whenever you're ready."

Yikes, what is he expecting me to say here? According to the cultist guidebook, Corinna is most interested in self-discovery. She wants to explore the labyrinth of her heart and figure out who she truly is. She wants to reshape reality so that she can experience authentic merriment. She wants Selanthian.

"Who am I?" I say. "What do I want?"

Ernie presses the stop button on the recorder.

"How was that?" I say.

He grins and presses the recorder against his chest in the same spot where he held the old book. He says, "Perfect."

ELEVEN

Later that day, Maggie returns from her honeymoon alone with claw marks on her left cheek that she received during a "psychic attack." At least that's what she calls it when she tells Nichelle, Cassian, Evangeline, and me the story. We're in the dining area, inhaling Atticus's coconut milk ice cream with homemade peanut butter cups mixed up inside.

"I didn't suspect anything at first," Maggie says. "Why would I? Ever since I've known him, Surfer likes to wake up early and wander around wherever he is, and it was the same at the beach house. In the beginning, nothing in his actions seemed out of the ordinary." Maggie holds her spoon out in front of her as she speaks, the ice cream dripping into her copper bowl. "But then he started acting distant. One moment, we'd be having a perfectly lovely conversation, and the next, he seemed ten thousand miles away. You know Surfer. He's not a bad listener. But he kept saying, huh, what, can you repeat that?" She lowers her spoon back into her bowl without taking a bite. "As the days went on, he came back later and later from his wanderings. He told me stories about what he saw and who he encountered. He spotted Elvis in a clock repair shop wearing a clown outfit. He overheard a guy who refused to look at photos of the sun because he was sure the image would harm his eyes. When Surfer told me these stories, he lacked his usual zeal. Do you know what I mean? He didn't move his arms around in his regular, vigorous way." She moves her hands around a little, mimicking Surfer's gestures. "All of this distance and weirdness led me to believe that something was terribly wrong. I asked him if he was experiencing some sort of crisis, and he acted stunned that such a thought would cross my mind." She sighs. "I wanted to believe that I was imagining things, but I could hear the guardians of my heart whispering the truth. And so, I woke up early one morning and went to look for him. Ordinarily, I can sense Surfer's presence and find him without much trouble. You've all seen this. In the park, I could always home in on his general direction. This time though, I couldn't feel him anywhere." And her voice breaks when she says, "He was hiding from me, on physical and metaphysical levels."

"That's terrible," Nichelle says.

"It took me forever," Maggie says. "But after hours of searching for him, I found him on the patio of a crab restaurant with some woman who looked almost exactly like me. At first I had this kind of out-of-body experience where I thought I was looking at one of my own memories. But the more I looked at the woman, the more I realized that she wasn't me. Her hair was too short. Her eyebrows were too thin. I thought about confronting the two of them right then and there, but I chickened out. I ended up watching them for a couple of minutes and then walking back to the beach house."

Maggie looks up from her ice cream, and her defeated-looking expression breaks my heart a little. She continues, "Surfer told me later that the woman is a movie producer named Gwenith. He said that he didn't mean to fall in love with her but that he had to follow his heart. Apparently, Surfer had seen her soul many times during his meditations at the park, and he mistook me for her. That's why he married me, he said. He thought I was her."

Maggie dabs at the corner of her eye with a fingertip.

"He did this on our freaking honeymoon," Maggie says. "It's too absurd to be real. And yet, here we are."

"He's a nincompoop," Evangeline says.

"He is," Maggie says. "This is what I get for giving my heart to a Gemini."

"Slander," Cassian says, under his breath, and Evangeline tells him to shush.

Maggie continues, "After telling me the truth, he packed up and left with her. I don't know where they went. Hollywood, probably. Don't you think? I stayed in the beach house, hoping that he'd come back and say that he'd made a big mistake. I could have forgiven him, I think. Probably. But he didn't return. And so I decided that I'd track him down and convince him to come to his senses. Sometimes he gets weird ideas in his head and he needs someone to help him see reason. You all know how he is." Maggie touches the claw mark on her left cheek. "After I made that decision, I fell asleep and someone made of bright light visited me in my dreams. She buzzed like a fluorescent bulb. She told me that she knew what I was planning, and that I should stay the frick away from Surfer and Gwenith. I tried to explain that I'd known Surfer for centuries. I told her that the fates wanted us to be together, and she responded by growling at me and attacking me. When I woke up, my cheek was bleeding." Absentmindedly, Maggie picks at one of her scabs. Moments later, she stops herself and places her hands palms-up on the table. There's a bit of blood on one of her fingertips. "I can't be sure exactly, but I think Gwenith's the one who attacked me in my sleep. When I first spotted her and Surfer talking together at that crab place, she emanated certain malevolent vibes. If I try to track them down, I'm sure she'll invade my dreams again. The scratches were only a warning. I'm thinking she's capable of much worse." She takes a deep breath.

"Obviously, there's a chance I scratched myself while I was asleep. But at the time, the woman made of light felt absolutely real and absolutely potent. So what exactly do I do now? Surfer's under the influence of some psychic succubus, or whatever the heck she is, and he needs my help. But what can I do? He thinks he's in love."

"I'm so sorry," Nichelle says.

Maggie looks around the table, as if searching our faces for answers. When her gaze shifts to me, I half-expect her expression to turn sour. There's a good chance, of course, that she doesn't want me here at this table. I'm a stranger to her.

However, her eyes and her eyebrows communicate only a pleading sort of vulnerability. Maybe she truly believes that the two of us were sisters in another life.

For a while, me and Nichelle and Evangeline and Cassian pepper her with a downpour of empathy and half-baked words of wisdom. Evangeline thinks that we should track down the producer and get a message to Surfer, warning him about Gwenith. Cassian thinks we should find a powerful psychic to battle the succubus, or whatever the hell she is. At first, Nichelle doesn't want to share her thoughts about the whole situation. But after some prodding, she tells us that she believes the woman of light might be an aspect of Maggie's own heart trying to warn her away from a toxic situation. When Maggie asks me what I think, I say, "I don't know."

Of course, that's not exactly true. I'm positive that we're not dealing with any sort of psychic phenomena. What we have here is an egocentric prick who left his wife for a movie producer because, based on what I've gleaned from my various conversations at the park, Surfer's obsessed with the idea of becoming famous. But I keep my mouth shut. According to the cultist guidebook, that's not an appropriate explanation for a mystical calamity.

Eventually, Maggie says, "The worst part about the whole

situation is that I could have prevented the whole mess if I'd spent more time at the park focusing on my passkey. But you know how I am. I can't sit still. I wasted my time here playing around."

"What happened isn't your fault," Nichelle says.

"How is it not?" Maggie says. "I neglected my labyrinth work, and now my life's as far from frickin' Selanthian as possible."

"I . . . the path toward authentic merriment can be treacherous at times for sure. It could be that Surfer's merriment wasn't compatible with your own, and so your paths diverged. I don't know." She places her hand on Maggie's again. "When you feel up to it, let's share what happened to you with Ernie and I'm sure he'll be able to offer you some helpful insights."

"Okay," Maggie says. "Not now though. I think right now I could use a nap." She stands and drums her fingers against the table. "You know what, my mind's racing too much for me to sleep right now. Maybe a meditation session at the energy center would do me some good. Would anyone want to join me?"

Nichelle and Evangeline and Cassian and I all agree to go with her.

On the way to the Mirror Maze, Maggie makes a bizarre yelping sound and points to our right. I scrutinize Doctor Owl's corkscrew-shaped alchemy lab. I see a crow hanging out on a crooked exhaust pipe that protrudes from the wall. I also see a polka-dot Ninja Turtle that someone's glued to a stained-glass window, so that the turtle appears to have six glass wings jutting out from his shoulders. None of this seems particularly yelp-worthy.

"Shit," Cassian says.

Shifting my gaze downward, I finally spot the dead raccoon on the track next to one of Doctor Owl's clockwork wagons.

The animal's sprawled on his back, his viscera spread out like bloody tentacles from his gaping torso.

After a few moments of silence, Cassian says, "The rodent-killer strikes again, huh?"

"A raccoon isn't a rodent," Evangeline says.

"Okay, well, the killer is mostly killing rodents. The dead rats we found were rodents. The possum in the lake was a rodent."

"A possum is a marsupial," Evangeline says. "I've told you that before, Cassian."

Nichelle takes a few steps closer to carnage, and grabs hold of the railing bordering the tracks. "Poor guy," she says.

Evangeline joins Nichelle at the railing and says, "Cassian and I saw a dog by the quarry the other day. Maybe he got in and did this."

"He was a coyote," Cassian says.

"He was too rotund to be a coyote," Evangeline says.

"So says you."

"I'll ask Cecil to recheck the outer walls," Nichelle says. "There must be an opening somewhere."

My heart right now is a tiny yellow hammer pounding at my chest. I've been waiting for someone to bring up the quarry in my presence.

"What's the quarry?" I say. "Is that the name of a ride I haven't seen yet?"

"No, it's an actual quarry," Evangeline says. "Cassian and I like to walk near it some mornings. It's beautiful. Well, the quarry itself isn't beautiful but it's a nice spot to take in the sunrise."

I'd like to pepper them with questions about the quarry, but that would probably come across as suspicious. A woman falls into a quarry and almost dies, and then the new recruit seems weirdly interested in that exact spot? "Hey, so, has anything terrible ever happened there?" I could say.

I let the topic drop for now. Later, I'll ask Evangeline if I can join her and Cassian on one of their sunrise walks. I doubt either of them had anything to do with Eff's fall, but going with them to the quarry would give me an opportunity to snoop around and ask some questions in a more organic way.

"Can we go now?" Maggie says.

Nichelle starts to say something, but I can't hear her because techno music pummels our ears from hidden speakers all around us. The Dredgers like to have these little impromptu dance parties every so often. Of course, no one in my little group joins in, because Maggie's frowning and standing perfectly still. Nichelle tells her something, her mouth almost touching Maggie's ear.

After a few seconds, we continue to the energy center. I perceive some movement in my peripheral vision, so I give the alchemy lab one last look. Someone in a goblin mask dances behind one of the soot-coated windows. I can only see their silhouette as they twirl and flail their arms. Below the window, the raccoon reaches toward the sky, screaming silently at the sun.

TWELVE

The next morning, I check up on Seraphina's life while the shower's running. Alvin's sent me a photo of Heracles wearing a small, glittery bowler hat. I text back and thank him again for everything he's done for me. Next, I call the hospital, and the doctor says what she always says, and I can feel my hand trembling when I place my phone next to the sink. Calling the hospital never gets any easier, even though nothing ever changes. Eff is in a coma. The hospital still doesn't know the severity of her brain injuries because the scans are imperfect tools. I feel as if the doctor and I are reading the same lines, again and again, every day. At the same time, things are changing. I can feel a timer counting down in my head. The longer Eff goes without regaining consciousness, the less likely it is that she ever will. Eventually, the timer's going to count down to zero, and the doctors will give up hope. They'll decide there's nothing more they can do.

After I shower and get dressed, I sit on my bed and take a few deep breaths, the way Eff taught me to years ago. I try to clear my mind of these gnawing, rotting thoughts.

I hate to admit this to myself, but a sense of relief spreads throughout my body as I ride the elevator down to the dining area. I'm looking forward to hanging out with whoever's still eating breakfast.

Back at the farmers' market, Nichelle told me that grieving is easier when you're surrounded by kind people, and she's right about that. I know someone here probably harmed Eff, but at this point I'm confident that there wasn't some grand conspiracy to hurt her. Most of these people seem harmless. They seem sweet. Sometimes, when I'm around them, I can hardly hear the ticking of the timer at all.

I eat, and chat, and meditate. I work on some fabric moths in the arts arena for the Selanight Revelries.

Eventually, I find myself following Nichelle into an oarless rowboat on a bromine-scented river full of brown water. We stuff our purses into the net pockets in front of us, and we pull the safety bar over our laps.

"Let me know if you notice any major malfunctions," Cecil says. "This is the maiden voyage, so the goblins might end up exploding for all we know." He clears his throat. "I'm kidding about that. Nothing will explode. Are you both comfortable?"

"Yep," Nichelle says.

"Snug as a bug," I say.

Cecil nods and walks over to position himself behind the boulder-shaped control panel.

"Bon voyage," he says, saluting us and leaving behind a smear of oil or grease or whatever on his forehead.

Suddenly, the boat lurches forward and we're floating toward the gaping, snaggy maw that leads into the goblin caverns. As we get closer, pus-colored fog spews from the cave opening.

Recently I researched the park on my phone a bit while sitting in the Keep's second floor bathroom. I read that a nine-year-old boy died on this ride a decade and a half ago when Goblintropolis was still open to the public. I found a few forum posts where people theorized about how exactly the boy died, but the news never released any specific details.

I try not to think too much about any of this while I'm actually riding the ride, and I'm definitely doing a great job so far, aren't I? We enter the cave, and dozens of rodent-like creatures dangle from the stalactites above, watching us with gleaming, azure eyes. A few of them open and close their lengthy muzzles, revealing rows of serrated teeth. Up ahead, a goblin stands near the waterway, wearing the same burlap cap as the head in the elevator. Maybe they're the same character.

While staring right at us, the goblin yanks at a tentacle, attempting to pull some creature out of a small crevice in the cave wall.

"What are you doing here?" the goblin says, and our boat reduces its speed to a slow crawl. "These caverns are no place for the likes of you. You seem brave, as far as humans go, but I doubt you're brave enough to face the creatures and cruelties ahead. You'd best turn back now while there's still time. Why not visit the old woman in the shoe and enjoy her freshly baked cinnamon bread? The bread's shaped like a foot, but they assure me it doesn't stink at all." He tilts his head to the side. "You refuse to turn back, eh? I must say I'm impressed by your fortitude. Good luck, humans. You're going to need it."

At this point, the goblin manages to wrench his prey out of the crevice, and the octopus smashes into his face, wrapping their tentacles around him.

"Blasted beast!" the goblin says.

Moving past the goblin, we glide through tortuous passageways, our boat twisting and turning around tight corners. Rusty sconces with emerald-green flames light our way. In time, we come to a long, straight stretch of tunnel with wine-red jewels or eggs or whatever they are embedded in the walls and ceiling. The eggs give off a faint glow, revealing the silhouettes of goblin babies squirming inside. White salamanders with giant eyes cluster around the egg jewels, as if basking in their light.

"So the goblins dig out their own children?" I say. "How does that work on a biological or evolutionary level?"

"It is pretty weird," Nichelle says. "Doctor Owl makes an appearance in a tunnel up ahead. You should ask him. He's a scientist."

"Isn't he an evil scientist?"

"Yeah, but he still graduated from an accredited university. Or, if you don't want to ask him, you could always read Binkler's ten-thousand-page, unpublishable manuscript. I think Ernie has a copy stored away somewhere. I hear the prose is dense and incoherent."

"Sounds great. I'll definitely do that."

We leave the luminescent babies behind and come to an area lousy with particularly large stalactites. Long-necked beetles crawl above us, using their mandibles to carve fractal patterns into the mineral formations. On our right, Doctor Owl sits in a wagon with a massive, spinning drill attached to one end. The owl's dressed in a leather lab coat, gripping a beaker with his clockwork, human-like hand. Bioluminescent worms wriggle inside the beaker.

"Very interesting," Doctor Owl says. "These might contain just the photoproteins I'm looking for."

Above the owl's head, a dozen or so beetles slowly lower themselves from the stalactites, using glittery green threads. The beetles open and close their razor-sharp-looking mandibles.

The owl laughs and says, "And to think, the witch we imprisoned told me today would be unlucky for me. What does she know anyway? She's nothing but a spud-brained charlatan."

As soon as the beetles touch the owl's head, he screams.

In the next section of the caverns, a spotlight shines down

on a six-foot spoon with googly eyes who's standing in front of a microphone. An audience of human-faced octopuses sit on the ground, facing the small stage.

"Oh my god," I say. "Nichelle."

She laughs in the dark beside me, and I laugh with her.

I can't believe she actually brought Spoon to life. No wonder she and Cecil both seemed so eager to get me to ride this thing.

"I hear those octopuses are a tough crowd," I say. "Spoon looks like he's killing it up there though."

"He definitely is," Nichelle says. "The octopi express amusement by staring straight ahead and grimacing. By the looks of it, they're all in stitches right now. They're loving the grandpa ladle material."

I sigh theatrically. "If only Spoon and Sunglasses Cat hadn't got in that big blow-up last night. Sunglasses should be here."

"It is a shame."

"Wait, who's that?" I say, and I pull the miniature Sunglasses Cat out of my purse. "Sunglasses, you old rascal. You made it."

I throw the stuffed animal at the stage, and he hits the wall and then lands next to an octopus that's gnawing on the head of a rodent.

We can't continue our little scene, because at this point, the boat turns a corner and we leave our anthropomorphic buddies behind.

In the darkness that now envelops us, I say, "You built a stage. You built a giant spoon."

"Cecil helped," Nichelle says.

"You are weird. Do you realize that?"

"Yep."

We progress through the ride, and we see worms with fuzzy antlers peeking out of holes in the walls and ceiling.

We see goblins mining for egg jewels. They place the eggs on embroidered cushions, and they dump diamonds and sapphires and emeralds into wooden barrels marked *TRASH*. The goblins sing a song about family that reminds me of all the cheesy ditties from the princess guidebook.

Our boat takes us into a dark passageway, and we can hear someone breathing. With every thunderous exhale, a burst of hot wind hits our faces. We then enter a gargantuan chamber bustling with slow-motion mayhem.

The Wolf King crouches on all fours as if ready to pounce, more massive than a city bus. All around him, the goblins languidly swing their pickaxes and shovels and tiny yellow hammers. One goblin swings an octopus around her head, as if preparing to chuck the cephalopod at her enemy. A few goblins grip the wolf's fur as they dangle from his body. Throughout all of this, the Wolf King appears completely unharmed and unfazed. He stares straight ahead at a mound of eggs, baring his bright white teeth with a cruel grin. He lets out a drawn-out, almost-melodious growl.

As the battle rages on, a horn-heavy orchestral piece swells and accelerates, pumped into the chamber from speakers I can't see.

"He's not as big as I thought he'd be," I say.

"Ha," Nichelle says.

Our boat meanders around the outskirts of the battle, giving us time to take in everything. Suddenly, some dark green mass breaks through the surface of the water right next to me, causing me to jump a little. The mass turns out to be a vine-like plant snaking out of the river, toward the stalactites above. Once the plant finishes rising, an amber-colored flower blooms toward the top, revealing a bulging, frog-like eye in the center of the petals.

More and more of these plants arise from the water. Some

of them watch the battle. Some of them stare at our boat and slowly track us as we float around.

We're nearing the end of this chamber when our boat stops with a modest jolt. I don't know why we're pausing here, but I face the battle, half-expecting some new development. Maybe the Wolf King will honor us with some Machiavellian speech. Maybe the goblins will deliver a killing blow to their tormentor. But nothing new happens.

"Are we supposed to be stalled here like this?" I say.

"I don't know," Nichelle says, almost too softly for me to hear.

We wait for a while longer, and the boat still doesn't budge.

"I think we're stuck," I say.

"I think you're right."

"Is there a camera in here somewhere? Can Cecil see us?"

"There is a control room with security monitors, but no one uses it."

"Wonderful."

I try to maneuver myself out of my seat, but the damned safety bar prevents me from freeing myself. Next, I grab my phone from my purse so that I can call the Dredgers' emergency landline. But there's no reception. Of course there's no reception.

I drop my phone back into my purse, and Nichelle stops pushing at the safety bar.

I say, "Cecil will notice eventually that we're not exiting the ride. Right?"

"Yeah," Nichelle says, once again barely audible.

I look at her. I study her face.

"Are you okay?" I say.

"Yeah," she says.

"Nichelle. You're not a good liar."

"Alright, yeah. I'm freaking out. It's a claustrophobia type thing. I'm not great on rides in general, but being stuck like this is next-level awful."

"Okay," I say, and I hold her hand. "Okay, let's go somewhere else. Close your eyes. Where should we go? To your Victorian mansion?"

"No," she says. "Not there. What about the beach?"

"Okay. The beach." I lean my head closer to hers so that I don't have to speak so vociferously to be heard over the music and the Wolf King's growls. "We're at the beach. We're both lounging on cat-print towels, because we're both unapologetic cat ladies. I'm wearing my red one-piece that I've had for a hundred years, and you're dressed in some cool one-shoulder swimsuit with a blooming water lily print. Your pendant's a piece of polished abalone shell. On our right, we can see a family of goblins. Some of them roast tentacles and salamanders over a green-flamed bonfire. Some of them pound on drums made from painted turtle shells, while others blow into horns made from dragon tusks. Goblin babies balance on the shoulders of the adults, holding their family members' hair to keep from falling. Babies on the sand dance little jigs."

"Aw," Nichelle says. "I like jigs."

"Yeah, I know," I say. "We can see Sunglasses Cat and Spoon out in the ocean, laughing and splashing each other. How Spoon can swim out there without any arms or legs, we're not exactly sure, but he's doing it. Spoon seems more confident and carefree than usual. Earlier today, he read a positive review of his comedy special in Human-Faced Octopus Magazine, and he's still riding that high."

"He deserves it," Nichelle says. "He's worked so hard."

The Wolf King snarls again, and I say, "Over on our left, my pet wolf's growling at a flock of seagulls. Stop terrorizing the animals, Artemis. I get up and fling her frisbee in order to distract her, and the frisbee veers off course and almost hits Cassian. Thankfully, he side-steps out of the way at the last second. I yell to him that I'm sorry, and he raises his hand and wiggles his fingers at me as if to say, don't worry about it. At least I hope that's what he means. He and Evangeline continue jogging together in their matching, lavender tracksuits. They sing a sea shanty duet about two old lighthouse keepers falling in love. Behind them, there's a sandcastle competition going on. Most everyone's sculpting a castle or a mermaid or a pirate ship, but we spot Topher constructing a sea monster with a hundred gnarled faces. While we're watching him work, my wolf growls again. Stop that, Artemis. Leave those winged rabbits alone. I throw the frisbee, as hard as I can, and the wind causes her beloved toy to veer off course again. This time around, the frisbee hits some guy in the back of the head. He goes down hard. When he gets up again, he looks around and we can finally see his face. It's Surfer, the cheating bastard. I look around for another frisbee to throw at him."

Nichelle laughs and opens her eyes.

"Feeling any better?" I say.

"Yeah," she says. "Thank you. My freakout-o-meter's down to a manageable two point nine. I can handle that."

"Let me know if it jumps up again, and I'll throw another frisbee at Surfer's head."

"For sure. I'll let you know." Nichelle looks at me, and I can see the emerald flames of the sconces flickering in her eyes. "You know, we should go to the beach for real sometime. I love the vibes of the ocean."

"We should definitely go," I say. "I have to warn you, though. Whenever I go to the ocean, I like to spend a good six hours searching for treasure with my metal detector. I hope you won't mind."

"That's funny, because whenever I go to the ocean, I like to spend a good six hours burying coins in the sand."

"Great, that sounds like a plan. We have the first six hours planned out. What do we do after that?"

Nichelle rests a finger against her cheek, like she does sometimes when she's thinking. "You can tell me stories by the bonfire. We can roast hot dogs. Veggie hot dogs."

I say, "We can dance by the fire like possessed marionettes."

"I don't dance," she says. "But I'll dance with you. Sorry, that was cheesy, wasn't it? I need to stop being so cheesy."

And I touch both sides of her face with my hands, and I pull her gently toward me. I kiss her. She kisses me back. I can feel the warmth of our imagined bonfire spreading in my chest. When was the last time I kissed someone I really like?

Nichelle pulls away from me, and she's smiling.

"I'm glad we did that," she says. "We should do it again."

"We should."

"Actually, wait. I need to come clean about something first."

"What? Please don't tell me you're a secret mime. I promised myself years ago I would never kiss a mime again."

Nichelle softly punches my shoulder. "This is serious. The thing is . . . I think it's my fault that we're stuck here like this. I didn't sabotage the ride directly, but I'm pretty sure I willed this whole boat malfunction scenario to happen."

I can tell when Nichelle's joking around, and her expression shows me that she's completely serious right now.

"I don't get what you mean," I say.

Nichelle bites at one of her fingernails. She says, "Things like this happen sometimes at the retreat. Reality bends to our wills, in subtle and not-so-subtle ways. I wanted to get closer to you, so I'm pretty sure the Silanthian energies trapped us here on purpose. I felt claustrophobic and freaked out, and this gave you an opportunity to show me once again how caring you are. And you kissed me. Things like this don't just happen to me unless Silanthian is involved, and I can for sure feel those energies in the air right now. So if I'm the reason we're stuck here, I'm sorry. I feel bad about trapping you like this."

"You didn't trap me," I say.

"Alright, maybe trapped isn't the right word. But my guilt-o-meter's reaching unhealthy levels, and I want you to accept my apology on the chance that I'm partially responsible for this."

I say, "Okay, and how do you know I'm not the one responsible? Maybe it's my will that broke the boat. I've been wanting to get closer to you too, you know."

Behind me, one of the goblins says, "Hi there." At least, that's who I think is speaking for a split second. But when I turn my head, I spot Cecil standing nearby, leaning against the Wolf King's front leg. "Need some help?"

After Cecil frees us from the safety bar, Nichelle and I hop the small gap over to the battleground. We weave our way through the animatronic pandemonium. As we avoid the swinging pickaxes and hammers and shovels, my own guilt-o-meter's reaching worrying levels. I know I'm not here at the retreat to kiss tall, beautiful, sweet people. Then again, what's wrong with me experiencing a little authentic merriment for once? Eff would approve. Anyway, there's no danger when it comes to getting closer to Nichelle. I'm sure she had nothing to do with what happened to George and Eff. Nichelle doesn't have a violent bone in her body.

We exit through the maintenance door, back into the much-too-bright light of day.

"I have to come clean about one more thing," Nichelle says. "I am a secret mime."

"Oh god no," I say.

After we say our goodbyes to Cecil, the two of us head toward the arts and crafts space. On the way, Nichelle wraps her arms around me and we kiss again, and for a few seconds, nothing else in the world matters.

THIRTEEN

It's initiation day, and while I'm having breakfast in the dining area, Maggie gives me a small opal that she says is the colors of my aura. Topher then tells me he adapted a scene from Binkler's manuscript that he got from Ernie about a goblin warrior and her true love, and he wants to act it out with me during the Selanight Revelries, if I'm interested. He places the script on the table next to the opal. Evangeline and Cassian and two other Dredgers sing me a song they wrote about Captain Corinna the Mighty Pirate. They sing a cappella, in the style of a barbershop quartet. It's embarrassing as all hell, and I have to fight not to hide my face while they're singing to me. Cecil whittled me a yawning housecat out of sycamore wood. Ernie says that he's noticed me admiring the crown of reeds in his giant's head, so he had a small pendant made, adorned with miniature acorns and pine cones and golden flowers. He says he spent hours holding the tiny crown and suffusing it with his hopes for my future. As Ernie clasps the gold chain around my neck, I think about Nichelle's many necklaces, and I wonder how many of them were gifted by Ernie. After everyone else is finished, Nichelle gives me a turquoise candle with a carving of my face that she tells me not to burn.

After breakfast, most of the Dredgers head for the stairwell. Nichelle and Ernie and I step into the elevator.

The goblin in the burlap cap opens his eyes and says, "Where's it to be? Floor two? Floor three? You seem formidable, as far as humans go, but I doubt you're tough enough to—"

I press the skull button.

"This must be some mistake," the animatronic says. "Surely you bumped the skull on accident. Certainly, a mere human lacks the courage necessary to press that button."

I press the skull again.

The goblin's eyes open wider for a moment. He says, "I must say I'm impressed by your valor. Now as we descend to the world below, I suggest you kiss your lucky rabbit's foot or pray to whoever it is humans pray to. You will need all the good fortune you can muster to make it through the many horrors of the Underbelly. Good luck."

The elevator door opens, and we enter the underground floor of the Keep. Someone's turned on all the arcade machines, so the digital zombies and other monsters form a chorus of screams and moans and howls. As I follow Ernie and Nichelle deeper into the Underbelly, I spot the Goblintropolis USA game. The glowing marquee looks as if it's splattered with blood. On the arcade monitor, the Wolf King sits on his throne, devouring goblin egg after goblin egg.

At the back of the Underbelly, the Dredgers gather around the entrance to a ride called *The Battle*. A winged rabbit-drawn carriage waits on the track, facing a dark tunnel that runs into the Underbelly wall.

Ernie and Nichelle lead me to the front of the crowd, so that we're standing beside the carriage.

Ernie says, "We're gathered here today to champion and to celebrate Corinna's initiation. She's warmhearted and hilarious. I'm sure we can all agree that she will be an indispensable addition to our little community. She belongs here, don't you think?"

The Dredgers cheer, and Topher unleashes one of his deafening whistles. Nichelle reaches over and squeezes my hand.

Ernie turns to me and says, "I can see that you're nervous, Corinna, and that's completely understandable. I wish I could alleviate your fears by telling you exactly what you're going to see and feel in there. However, each one of us experiences the initiation in a different way." He places his hand on the open eye of the winged rabbit. "What I can tell you is that this is a sacred space here at the park. I've spent countless hours sitting inside this ride, meditating, opening doors to the Selanthian realm, allowing the energies to permeate the area. Due to the potency of this power, you are not under any circumstances to get off your carriage and linger inside the ride. Your visit must remain brief."

At this point, Ernie pulls a plastic bag out of his pocket, which contains a lumpy brown ball about the size of a human eye.

He says, "Traditionally, before entering the ride, the initiate eats one of my specially made bezoars. You're probably thinking, 'what the hell, Ernie?' You're thinking, 'isn't a bezoar a ball of hair that collects in the gastrointestinal system of a cow?'"

A few of the Dredgers laugh.

"Well, this isn't an actual bezoar," Ernie says. "In actuality, it's a mixture of dates and mushrooms that I've imbued with Selanthian energies. Eating it will help open your mind to the other realm."

"It's safe," Nichelle says. "But it's up to you whether you eat it or not."

Ernie opens the bag and pulls out the ball. He holds it out to me.

I'm a little freaked out, but I can feel eyes of all the Dredgers on me. I need them to trust me. I need to prove to them that I trust them. I need them to accept me.

Nothing at the park has done me any harm so far, so I doubt this bezoar is any more dangerous than their mystical circles and triangles. Maybe when Ernie says the bezoar's made of dates and mushrooms, he means magic mushrooms. I can handle that.

I take the ball, leaving a bit of the outer goop stuck to his fingers.

When I bring the bezoar to my mouth, I can smell roses and wet dog and rot. Thankfully, the brown ball predominantly tastes like dates and mushrooms. Nevertheless, the ball leaves behind an aftertaste of sickly-sweet decay on my tongue.

"Perfect," Ernie says. "Now let's give the energies in the bezoar some time to work their way through your system. Let's sit and focus our thoughts on Corinna and her journey."

So for a while, we all sit and meditate. After thirty minutes or so, I start feeling a little light-headed.

Ernie says, "I think you're ready."

We all stand, and Nichelle hugs me and says, "Everything will be fine."

Opening the carriage door, Ernie says, "Your life, in all its intricacies, has led you to this moment." He gently squeezes my shoulder.

I sit inside my carriage, and as soon as it lurches forward, the Dredgers cheer again. In a moment, I'm swallowed up by the tunnel in the wall. And then I'm soaring on my carriage through a dazzlingly blue sky. The bezoar has definitely taken effect, because I feel as if I'm truly floating. Hundreds of goblins glide through the sky with me, most of them depicted in murals painted on the walls. They ride on rabbit-drawn carriages and chariots and wagons. Some of them ride their rabbits bareback. In addition to all the creatures in the murals, there are also a few animatronics soaring beside me. The goblin with the burlap cap stands on his chariot, holding a massive pickaxe. He looks at me and smiles weakly. Suddenly, the track slopes downward, and I'm descending slowly through a crowd of violet clouds. I'm descending toward a miniature castle, featuring dozens of jagged spires. A glass tower in the center of the castle rises higher than any other structure. Inside the glass tower, hundreds of golden gears turn endlessly. Even from here in the sky, I can hear the Wolf King growling.

Before reaching the miniature castle, my carriage veers to the right, and I pass through another tunnel and find myself in an open field with the goblin army. We race forward, toward the distant, gnarled wall of the Wolf King's castle. The goblins yell out their battle cries. I veer to the left and pass through another tunnel, and we're closer to the outer wall now. All around me, goblins swing their hammers and pickaxes and shovels, battling massive monstrosities with badger bodies and owl heads. Each monster has a cluster of eyes covering its face with a serrated metal beak in the center. The monsters are covered with fur, aside from the glass covering their stomachs, revealing the moving clockwork and squirming organs within. Nearby, Doctor Owl stands in his flying contraption, gazing down calmly at the battlefield. Everything here looks more detailed than in the previous sections of the ride. Everything sounds louder. I know only the animatronics are capable of movement, but the figures in the wall murals are twitching now as well. The goblins scream.

I pass through another tunnel, and the battlefield is dappled with dead or dying goblins. Doctor Owl's still in his flying machine, now reading a book. Near me, the goblin with the burlap cap lies motionless on the ground, staring unblinking at the sky. The giant monstrosities curl up together on a patch of grass, snoring peacefully as they sleep. Inside their stomachs, I can see chunks of flesh winding their way through the gears of their clockwork innards.

Another tunnel later, and I'm still on the battlefield, heading straight for the eyeball tree. The cadaverous-looking hands at the ends of the branches reach toward me. The many jaundiced eyes of the tree stare at me. The mouths open wide, exposing their kaleidoscopic fangs, and the mouths remain open. Around me, luminous phantoms the color of the sky drift toward the open mouths. These must be the souls of the goblins who died on the battlefield. I shudder when I spot my own face through the veil of one of the phantoms. Am I seeing this because of the bezoar, or did the other Dredgers set this up?

Phantom after phantom gets swallowed by the tree.

I get closer and closer, and sometimes I feel as if I'm moving through time faster than usual, and sometimes slower.

As I enter one of the gaping maws, I can hear the Wolf King howling with laughter.

I'm inside now. My carriage travels at a snail's pace through the colossal cylindrical chamber inside the tree. I can't see the tracks anymore because the floor's covered by a sea of yellow-green fog. In every direction, amorphous formations of sap-coated wood protrude up from the fog and down from the ceiling. Phosphorescent body parts jut out of the formations. I spot the goblin with the burlap cap. He's trapped in one of the anomalous structures, save for one arm and half his head. His fingers twitch. His one visible eye rolls around aimlessly in his head. Above him, a goblin woman dangles from one of the ceiling formations, her head entrapped entirely in the wood. Her body wriggles. The souls stuck in this tree moan and groan and wheeze. I'm feeling nauseous, and a little dizzy. All of a sudden, the lights flash on and off, on and off, faster and faster.

The faces poking out of the formations begin to change. Sometimes they're human, and sometimes they're goblin, and sometimes they're some combination of both. I see a man with amber eyes and teeth made from shards of multicolored glass. As his one free arm stretches toward me, pale twigs shoot out from his fingertips.

What is this place? What am I doing here? I think I'm on some sort of ride, but I can't recall getting in this carriage. I feel dizzy.

"Who am I?" my own voice says, from somewhere above me.

I look up and flickering lights overwhelm my eyes. I look down again.

"Who am I?" my voice says again.

Seconds pass, and I can't remember my name. I laugh, because who the fuck doesn't remember something like that? The idea is absurd.

Corinna. Seraphina. I'm Seraphina. I remember everything again. This is my initiation.

"Who am I?"

Ah, this is my question from the recording Ernie and I made in the giant's head. He must be playing my voice using a hidden speaker above me. Or am I actually speaking out loud? I keep my right hand on my mouth to make sure my lips aren't moving.

"Who am I?"

Yeah, my lips aren't moving. This must be the recording. What are they expecting me to do in here?

I glance around the chamber, and I see my dad's head sticking out of the wood, his eyes sunken, his open mouth packed with leaves. He turns his head back and forth, over and over. He moves so fast that he becomes a blur. A few flashes of light later, he's a goblin again.

I turn my gaze to the fog. If I keep scanning the formations,

I afraid that I'll recognize more people trapped in the wood. Everyone's here, I think.

"What do I want?" I ask. "What do I want? What do I want? What do I want?"

What I want is to get the fuck out of here and find Nichelle. I'm sick of this place.

"What do I want? What do I want?"

When I look up from the fog, I see a woman made of bright golden light standing near my carriage. At first, I can only perceive a few vague details in regard to her form. After a few seconds though, my eyes adjust I guess, and I can make out the delicate-looking glass that acts as her skin. She's grinning at me, her expression warped with malevolence. She buzzes.

I know her somehow, I think.

Where?

The lights flash. The air smells pungently of Selanthian energies.

Oh, this is the woman from Maggie's dream. What is she doing here?

"What do I want?" I ask again, from above. "What do I want? What do I want? What do I want?"

The glass woman points at me with a long, blade-like finger, and she speaks in grating bursts of static sounds. I don't think she'll let me go until I answer the question.

What I want is what I've always wanted since I was a small, shattered girl. I lost my dad, and I lost Aunt Gloria, and I lost my mom in a different way. Eff might be next. I could teach a master class in pushing people away, but I'm tired of being like this. I'm tired. The glass woman glows brighter and brighter, and the static wails in my ears, and I feel as if I'm burning away.

FOURTEEN

Early in the morning, Cassian and Evangeline and I exit the park through the back gate. We're carrying flashlights, although the frail illumination of twilight is growing brighter with every passing moment.

"I'm glad you decided to join us," Evangeline says. "It really is a lovely spot."

"I'm glad too," I say.

For no real reason at all, I always imagined the quarry bordering a forest of ponderosa pines and incense cedars and white firs. In reality, we're facing an overgrown field flecked with dandelions. A ways away, a rusty sedan protrudes above a cluster of tall grass, and a neon-green penguin sits on the roof. When she was a girl, Eff used to leave stuffed animals all over the place. I remember her tossing a doll on top of Aunt Gloria's refrigerator and arranging a family of monkeys in dad's favorite oak tree. Is there a chance Eff left the neon penguin on this car? Is she the one who left all the stuffed animals on the carousel in the park? None of this matters, I guess, but I can't help searching for signs of her wherever I look. Side-by-side-by-side, the three of us jog along a serpentine trail of blackened, trampled weeds. Someone must have burned this path through the field, and I'm picturing Topher in his goblin mask, wielding his trusty blowtorch.

How exactly he prevented the fire from spreading throughout the field, I'm not at all sure.

After a while, I become aware of a faint humming sound that intensifies the closer we get to the quarry. The sound reminds me of the woman made of glass and light. I can't remember everything I saw during the initiation, but I remember her.

Cassian wiggles his fingers in the direction of an old smudge pot in the field with a cowboy hat on top. He says, "Wasps."

"Bees," Evangeline says. "I don't know why you insist on acting like Steve Irwin when you have no real interest in zoology or animals in general."

"I am not acting like Steve Irwin," Cassian says.

The coquettish battle rages on until the two of them start singing some 1920s-sounding duet about a runaway train. They try to get me to sing choo-choo-choo with them in harmony during the chorus. I refuse.

The scorched path leads us closer and closer to the massive hole in the earth, and my heartbeat thuds in my ears. Before we get very close, Evangeline and Cassian stop and sit on a couple of flat boulders. The sunrise is blooming on the horizon.

I take a deep breath. I need to sound as nonchalant as possible.

I don't know if this is going to work, but I start walking toward the quarry and say, "I'm going to sit on the edge."

"Wait," Evangeline says. "It's dangerous."

"I'll be fine," I say.

"Corinna, stop. It's not safe. Someone fell in there recently. One of us. Please come back."

After taking another deep breath, I turn around and head back toward them.

"That's horrible," I say, and I sit on one of the flat boulders beside them. "Who fell? Are they Okay?"

The two glance at each other, and Evangeline says, "A woman named Eff fell before you came here. She liked to take late-night walks by herself. Four-in-the-morning late. Thank Selanthian Cassian and I wanted to walk around the quarry that day, because we're the ones who spotted her. She wasn't going to last long down there without emergency care. The last we heard, she's still in a coma."

"How did I not hear about this before now?" I say.

Evangeline remains silent for a few moments and then says, "Ernie thought we shouldn't burden you with a tragedy when you were first settling in. The early days here are challenging and confusing enough, as I'm sure you'd agree. You didn't need a whole catastrophe added to your plate."

"Also, you know how the park works," Cassian says. "Focusing on Eff's fall would only spread negativity and drive away the Selanthian energies we're trying to cultivate here. It's better, for all our sakes, to focus on all the positives that she brought to our lives." Evangeline turns to her partner and says, "Cass, don't let us forget to ask Maggie for an update on Eff during breakfast. She's been so preoccupied with the wedding and the honeymoon and the succubus, she hasn't told us anything for a while."

Cassian scratches the back of his neck and says, "I'm sure if Eff were out of her coma, she wouldn't forget to tell us."

Evangeline says, with annoyance saturating her voice, "I'm still interested in hearing about any minor changes. Aren't you?"

"Yes, dear," he says. "You're right. As always."

I search their faces, and I don't know exactly what I'm looking for. Maybe some indication that they're keeping something from me? I don't think they're lying about any of this.

So Maggie and Eff were close, apparently. Maybe Maggie knows something about the night Eff fell. I need to talk with her.

"Do you mind if we meditate here for a while?" Evangeline says. "Whenever we come here, we like to dispel some of the negative vibes still lingering in the air. I think Eff would appreciate that. She loved this place."

"I don't mind," I say, and while the two of them meditate, I close my eyes and think about what I'm going to say to Maggie.

Afterward, we begin our walk together around the quarry, careful not to get too close to the edge. We don't say anything for a while. Eventually, Cassian points out the location where they spotted Eff, and I don't want to look, but I have to. She fell so far. In my mind's eye, I can see her broken body curled up down there.

I turn away. I'm sorry, Eff. I'm sorry this happened to you.

We walk, silently again.

Maybe I'll return here by myself soon and search for clues. I'm sure I'll be able to find a damning piece of evidence that a bunch of trained officers couldn't spot. Sure, sounds perfectly plausible.

We continue making our way around the quarry, but no matter how far we go, the hole in the world never seems to end.

FIFTEEN

In the morning, the phone call to the hospital leaves me as crushed as usual, and I'm wallowing in my misery until Nichelle walks over to the dining table and kisses the top of my head.

"I've been practicing my mime work," Nichelle says. "Do you want to see?"

"No, I do not," I say.

She mimes that she's blowing up a balloon, and then she slowly swallows the balloon.

"I hate this," I say.

"But it's fun."

"Mimes don't talk, Nichelle."

After breakfast, a few of us head to the Haunted Forest where Topher and I practice his script about the goblin lovers.

"I don't know how to do this," I say. "I don't know how to say goodbye to you. I tried composing some poems for you, but they were inadequate. I've burned them and buried them in the woods"

"You shouldn't have done that, man," Topher says.

The scene progresses, I haven't felt this comfortable acting in I-don't-know-how-many-years.

Later in the day, I make my way across the drawbridge that leads to the Wolf King's Dungeon. To my right, a rodent-faced sea serpent greets me by rising out of the moat and roaring as a cluster of tentacle-like tongues squirm out of his gaping jaws. The many badger ears growing out of the creature's back twitch and tremble. Whenever I come this way with Nichelle, she likes to walk over and pat the sea serpent's belly.

I continue forward and pass under the entryway. Instead of traditional spikes, the portcullis has multicolored goblin teeth fused to the bottom of the gate. They shine a kaleidoscope of light all around me as I pass over the threshold into the dungeon.

Inside, I glance around the dim, torchlit prison until I spot Maggie on an exercise bike. She's wearing gray yoga pants and a t-shirt with a spectral horse and carriage on the front. Next to Maggie, a winged rabbit tilts his head and watches her. Every few seconds, the rabbit's eyes blink, but his bewildered expression never changes. I feel a sudden, absurd urge to set the animatronic free from the metal chains attached to his legs.

"Hi," I say.

"Hello, sweetheart," Maggie says, sounding more than a little out of breath.

I climb onto the exercise bike beside her. Near me, a goblin woman in a burlap tunic gnaws at the bars of her small iron cage. Her tiny baby sits on her shoulder, gazing at me with enormous eyes.

Maggie slows her pace a little and says, "Did I tell you I saw the succubus again? I was awake this time. Can you believe that? I was walking back to my room from the energy center, and I had a sudden overpowering impulse to get in my car and drive to Los Angeles to find Surfer. But then I spotted Gwenith in the window of that little food stand shaped like a giant shoe. She was made of light, just like in my dream." Maggie slows her pedaling even more. "She didn't say anything, but I could tell what she was thinking. She emanated some fairly menacing vibes. She didn't want me driving off to search for Surfer." She coughs a few times, and sweat streams down her face, but she doesn't wipe any of it away. "Obviously, there's a chance that what I saw was a trick of the light, but I don't think so. The light had a distinctly feminine form—okay, Maggie, stop. No more headspace for Surfer and his movie producer. Let's talk about literally anything else."

"Okay," I say.

For a while, we pedal in silence, side-by-side. On the other side of the gym, someone in a goblin mask positions himself on a tilted stretching rack so that his head's close to the floor. With his feet anchored to the torture device, he performs some rapid, painful-looking sit-ups.

I look at Maggie. She's still glistening with a veneer of sweat.

I clear my throat and say, "I was jogging with Evangeline and Cassian by the quarry. They told me what happened to your friend. What a horrible accident. I'm sorry."

"Thank you," Maggie says, in a quiet tone that makes her not sound like Maggie at all.

"How is Eff doing?"

"She still hasn't regained consciousness. Apparently, she's not recovering as quickly as they'd hoped, but I'm positive things will turn around soon. I've always felt that Eff's destined for great things. I think she has much more to do here in this realm before she moves on."

"I hope you're right." I'm not sure how Maggie will respond to the deluge of bullshit I'm planning to release, but this is the best idea I've got. "Something strange happened to me when we were at the quarry."

Maggie glances at me inquisitively and says, "Yeah?"

"Yeah," I say, and my mouth's suddenly dry, as if I've swallowed a handful of hot beach sand. "Evangeline and Cassian and I were meditating beside the quarry, trying to banish the negative vibes from there. And I don't know exactly how to explain it, but I felt as if some of the energy at the quarry was calling out to me, like there was a message that needed to be heard. So I opened myself up and took some of that energy inside me."

Maggie stops pedaling and says, "That isn't safe, Corinna. You have to guard yourself in negative spaces like that."

"Well, I was curious. So I examined the energy and I perceived fragments of images. I saw a man getting hit by a car, and I saw Eff falling. I think Eff left these psychic imprints behind so that we could understand what happened to her."

Maggie's eyes open wide. "Eff's ex was injured in a hit-and-run," she says.

"Do you know of any connection between the hit-and-run and what happened at the quarry?"

"I . . . don't know. I don't think so. All I know about the whole hit-and-run situation is that Eff was having visions about George with broken pieces of glass in his face and a bone coming out of his arm. When Eff received proof that George was in a hit-and-run, she freaked out. She thought Atticus might have been responsible. I was there with her when she confronted him, and he proved that he was nowhere near George when the hit-and-run happened. He was across the country. Eff seemed satisfied by that." Maggie sighs. "I thought Eff was done freaking out, but later, she sat me down and told me some fairly outlandish stuff. Nonsense."

"What kind of nonsense?"

"She was struggling, emotionally and spiritually, and she convinced herself that she was responsible for what happened to George. Can you believe that? She thought that the energies here were tapping into her buried impulses, like her subconscious desire for George to get what's coming to him. Obviously, I told her that Selanthian energies don't work like that. They only reshape reality to achieve positive outcomes. You can't just subconsciously will someone to get hit by a car." She moves her hand in front of her, as if it's a car passing her face. "This sort of spiritual crisis isn't a super common occurrence at the park, but it does happen. Dealing with multiple realities and mystical powers can be confusing and disorienting. Right? I told her to talk with Ernie and Nichelle, because usually those two can set a Dredger in crisis straight and explain the true meaning of Selanthian. Once or twice, a confused Dredger has left the retreat permanently, but that's a rarity. Ernie and Nichelle know what they're doing."

"Did Eff talk with Ernie and Nichelle?"

"I don't know. Probably." She rubs her at the corner of her eye with a finger. "So that's the whole of the hit-and-run situation. I can't see how any of this might connect with Eff's accident. Do you really think there's a connection?"

"Maybe. The vision's difficult to interpret."

"Alright, I'm below empty," Maggie says, climbing off her bike. "I didn't get much sleep last night, and I could use a nap. Let's definitely continue this conversation later though, sweetie."

I get off my bike and walk with Maggie to the entrance of the dungeon. Under the portcullis, patches of multicolored light shine on her face, making rainbows of the scratches on her cheek. She hugs me. Then she says, "If Eff sent us a psychic message, and it sounds like she did, we'll figure out what she wanted us to know. We will."

"Definitely," I say.

As Maggie saunters away, the rodent-faced sea monster bellows above her head and she winces a little.

Next, I head into the energy center so I can stare at my little circles and think for a while. What did I learn from my conversation with Maggie? Eff was having some sort of spiritual crisis. Does that have anything to do with her fall? Should I investigate the Atticus angle further or would that be a waste of time? Atticus seems harmless to me, and he apparently proved to Eff that he was nowhere near the hit-and-run when it happened. But what if he fabricated the evidence in order to throw Eff off his trail? God, I don't know what the fuck I'm doing. I know I need to look deeper into Eff's crisis of faith. Maggie said Eff probably spoke with Ernie and Nichelle, but does that mean anything? Anytime anyone ever has a spiritual problem or question, they go to Ernie and Nichelle. I need to think more about this. I need to spend some time preparing questions and tactics. Right now, I'm hungry, so I head to the dining area and I devour Atticus's shaved brussels sprout salad and whole-wheat rigatoni with kale pesto. This might sound a bit terrible, but Atticus can even make kale taste delicious.

"Corinna," Evangeline says. "We're trying to remember how many golf balls Alan Shepard left on the moon. Do you remember? Can you settle this for us?"

"Sure," I say. "I'd love to get in the middle of one of your arguments. That sounds like a lot of fun."

"It's three," Cassian says.

"Two," Evangeline says.

I say, "You're asking the right person, because I remember everything about Shepard's Apollo mission. They built an entire miniature golf course on the moon. There are dozens of balls, and a little windmill, and a skull at the end of the course with a mouth that opens and closes."

"You're no help," Cassian says.

The great debate carries on, and I turn my attention away from my table.

On the other side of the dining area, Nichelle stands with her head tilted to the side as she draws bizarre diagrams on the massive marker board mounted to the wall. She's wearing a sleeveless gray top and those white-and-gray striped shorts that show off how awe-inspiring her legs truly are. I can't see her face from here, but I know she's bunching her lips almost imperceptibly to one side, the way she always does when she concentrates.

I know I need to speak with her about Eff, but I don't know yet what approach I should use. What new lies should I tell her? I wish I didn't need to deceive her this way.

But I'll think about all this more tomorrow. Right now, I'm the sort of mentally exhausted where I'm likely to slip up if I try to do more detective work.

When Nichelle notices me looking at her, she abandons her Selanthian diagrams and takes her usual spot next to me at the table.

"Did you hear the news?" Nichelle says. "Spoon booked a role in a sitcom pilot. He's going to play the wacky soup spoon who lives across the hall."

"That old trope," I say.

"He and Sunglasses are pretty excited. They're hosting a party tonight in a kitchen cabinet. They said we could come if we want to, and if we can figure out how to fit inside a cabinet."

"That's no problem for me. Did I ever tell you I'm a professional contortionist?"

"Oh no. I promised myself years ago I would never kiss another contortionist."

We go on and on like this, all the way up to our room.

When I fall asleep, I find myself sitting cross-legged on a patch of mowed grass that borders a forest of yellowish-brown, leafless trees. I examine the oaks closest to me. A pair of goblins perch on nearby branches, snacking on skewered salamanders and bioluminescent insects. A baby goblin hops from branch to branch in pursuit of a pink moth. Another goblin dangles upside-down from one of the trees. He watches me with kind, twinkling eyes.

"We should go home," Eff says, her body small and elfish, now sitting cross-legged in front of me.

"Not yet," I say. "Let's stay for a little while longer. We're on a planet filled with talking flowers. How should we defeat the giant killer gopher? What weapons do we have?"

Eff sighs and her eyes and nose and mouth lurch impossibly to the side of her face. When her face returns to normal, she says, "We're not supposed to be here."

"This is a park, isn't it?" I say. "This is a public space. We have just as much a right to be here as anyone else."

Eff turns her head backward, farther than she should be able to turn it.

"Don't do that," I say.

I'm standing beside Eff now, and we're both scrutinizing the trees. The goblins stare at us with unblinking eyes and frozen grins. The wind groans. A goblin in a burlap cap teeters on his branch and falls flat on the grass, right next to a brontosaurus-shaped slide. I look up at the baby goblin I spotted earlier, and he's suspended in the air by an almost-invisible metal wire. He's reaching out for a fabric butterfly that's also attached to a wire.

I thought as long as the goblins were watching over us, we would be safe here. But they're nothing more than cardboard cutouts. Why did I think they were alive?

I glance over and Eff's still standing beside me, only she's older now. She takes a long drag of her vape pen and exhales a neon-green cloud that hovers between us for a few seconds before floating away.

"I keep pulling out teeth," Eff says. With two fingers, she wiggles at one of her front teeth until it comes loose. She swallows the tooth a moment later.

"You probably shouldn't eat them," I say.

"That's your opinion."

I can hear someone stepping on the fallen, crunchy leaves

in the forest, but I can't see anyone yet. It's probably our mother coming to take us back home.

Eff takes another drag of her vape pen, and her eyes jerk to the sides of her face and settle below her ears. When she returns to normal, she says, "I snooped around and looked at Doctor Owl's papers. He has a fucked-up mind, Phina. I think he's created something awful. You should go."

Suddenly, someone hurtles out of forest and into the park, and it's not our mother at all. The man reaches toward us with numerous mangled fingers sewn to each of his hands. Someone's removed his head from his neck, but a dozen or so faces protrude from his elongated torso. The faces look ashen and withered and dead.

I look over and Eff's body has fallen into pieces.

I try to move and I try to scream, and all the man's mouths open impossibly wide, as if he's unhinged his jaws like a snake.

SIXTEEN

On the morning of the Selanight Revelries, we all bustle around the park, putting up decorations, removing a whole section of artificial grass in the Haunted Forest, building a makeshift stage from sheets of old plywood, preparing food and drinks, and on and on. We're coated with sweat, because today's unseasonably blistering, and Maggie, our resident event coordinator, is bellowing out orders with a megaphone that she doesn't even need. Setting up a merriment festival is fucking hard work, but we're having fun, nonetheless. Some of us start drinking early.

After lunch, we all pile into the Mirror Maze, and when I say 'all,' I mean every single Dredger residing at the park. We're so packed in here that we have to sit three or four to a cubicle. I'm in a cubicle with Nichelle and Evangeline and Cassian, and when Ernie gives the word, we all focus on our passkeys simultaneously. We're meant to concentrate on drawing more Selanthian energies into the park so that our merriment tonight will be intensified. As Nichelle explained to me earlier with her markerboard and diagrams, human beings aren't meant to physically exist in dense Selanthian fields for an extended period of time, and so we limit these experiences to festival days and initiations. After tonight, the energies will dissipate and return to tolerable levels. I barely understand any of this, but I like how excited Nichelle gets when she explains things to me.

While we're focusing on our passkeys, Topher starts laughing in a nearby cubicle. He snorts uncontrollably when he laughs, and this causes Cassian to chuckle. Evangeline giggles. The snowball keeps rolling, and soon enough, every Dredger is cracking up. Laughter isn't an uncommon occurrence in the energy center, but this is next-level.

Once everyone quiets down, Nichelle mimes applying broom-length lashes to her eyes and fluttering them at me flirtatiously. I mouth at her, "Stop it."

In my head, I start to brainstorm some ideas for who I should speak to next about Eff, but in no time at all, everyone's piling back out of the energy center. We flit about, finishing up the preparations. At one point, Topher offers me a small piece of bezoar. He says, "Microdosing this stuff will give you a way different experience than the initiation, man. Take this much, and you'll just float around and some of the animatronics might smile at you." I'm a little tempted, but for now I decide to stick with Atticus's homebrew.

Everything's so hectic and loud, I decide to spend the rest of the festivities as Corinna. I'll let Seraphina and her scheming and anxieties take a break for once.

Once the sun sets, the Selanight Revelries begin.

Everyone gathers at the Haunted Forest, and I grab two pink and yellow cocktails with a sign nearby that reads *The Rosy Maple Moth*. I hand one of the drinks to Nichelle.

"I think Cassian invented this," Nichelle says.

"Oh great," I say. "He always shows so much restraint and common sense when creating new things. Do you think there are actual moths crushed up in this?"

"Probably."

I take a sip of the cocktail, and it's surprisingly tolerable. I can't detect even a hint of insect.

We head over toward Evangeline and Cassian and a few others standing among the pale trees of the Haunted Forest. Everyone's wearing feathery antennae of various colors. Glowing blue phantoms dangle from the branches above us, showing off their new cheesecloth wings embedded with fairy lights. Hundreds of aluminum moths made from soda cans also inhabit the trees. Thanks to the blacklight paint we applied over the last few days, the aluminum moths glow in brilliant neon colors, their wings displaying patterns of overlapping circles and triangles and other shapes.

"What do you think?" Cassian says, wiggling his fingers at the cocktail in my hand.

"Ambrosial," I say.

"I told you people would like it," Cassian says to his other half.

"She's only being nice," Evangeline says.

We chat for a while, and before long, Topher comes over and tells me it's time. We head over to the stage we built next to the eyeball tree. Earlier today, we wrapped the eyeball tree in dyed cotton batting so that the monstrosity now looks like a massive pink cocoon. Topher and I apply green makeup to each other's faces.

All the Dredgers gather around, and we put on our little production about the goblin huntress and her true love.

Toward the end of the scene, Topher says, "You're acting like this is our last goodbye."

"The regiment's assaulting the Wolf King's castle," I say. "You think this attack will be different from all the others? We've trained as well as we can, but we're not warriors."

"You have . . . you have tenacity. You have heart, man."

"Heart doesn't win wars."

Topher cries now, and I approach him slowly and wrap my arms around him. "You're right. You are. Maybe things will be different."

Topher keeps crying.

"I'll come back to you," I say. "I'll try my best to come back to you."

When the scene ends, the audience applauds. Ernie gives me a double thumbs-up. Carly tosses a bouquet of silk moths onto the stage.

I return to the crowd, and Nichelle takes my hands and says, "That was fantastic."

"Thanks," I say. "Okay, now it's your turn. I've told everyone you're doing two hours of mime on stage tonight. I hope you're ready."

"Of course I am," Nichelle says. "Two hours is nothing. I could do three easily."

"Great."

Next, we head over to that section at the center of the Haunted Forest where we removed the artificial grass. Here, we light our bonfire. I see a couple people placing bits of bezoar on each other's tongues. We eat moth-shaped cookies, and on moth-shaped papers we write down people and objects and ideas that are keeping us from authentic merriment. We toss our papers into the flames. Some Dredgers throw in photographs. After we're done burning things, Topher tells a story about the moth man creeping into an old man's bedroom at night and eating the man's hair. Nichelle tells me that she likes to spend the end of every Selanight meditating and writing on her tuffet, and she asks me if I want to join her when the time comes. Of course I say yes. Evangeline and Cassian and the rest of the barbershop quartet sing a song about Mothra. Eventually, Cecil and Ocean and the rest of the Dredgers folk rock group carry their instruments onto the stage. They don't sing about moths, but nobody cares. They're good. Cecil's a fucking virtuoso on the guitar. I dance with Nichelle by the bonfire, and I can see the fervent flames reflected in her eyes. At one point, Ernie cuts in and while we dance, he leads me away from the fire. He leans in close to my ear and says that we need to have a conversation about Nichelle when we get the chance. He says there are things I need to know. I say, "Okay." The song ends after that and he lets me go. I'm anxious about Ernie's words, of course, but as soon as I return to Nichelle and she puts her arms around me, I don't worry so much anymore. We keep dancing. If I believed in Selanthian energies, that would explain the magic in the air.

Late into the night, all the Dredgers follow a trail of tiki torches across the park. Cecil and Ocean have spent countless hours rebuilding the Goblin Chapel, and Ernie thought Selanight would be the perfect time for us to experience the grand reopening. On Selanight we're meant to honor our inner children, and apparently Ernie spent a lot of time at the Chapel as a kid.

We approach the entrance of the building, and everything's illuminated by high-powered floodlights. Pudgy vines cover the outside walls, specked with bright yellow flowers with frog-like eyes in the center of the petals. The eyes move in random directions. Goblin statues stand on both sides of Selanthian-inscribed doors, dressed in rough-spun gowns the same vibrant yellow as the flower petals. The goblins are grinning, their glass teeth glistering in the powerful beams of the floodlights. With outstretched arms, they usher us forward. Was there a bit of bezoar in that cookie I ate earlier? I'm feeling a little floaty.

Ernie pulls open the door and we make our way into the building, and we're now inside one of the goblin caverns. Rows of reddish-brown pews stretch out ahead of us. Above us, rodent-like creatures hang from stalactites, their wrinkly babies clinging to their long woolly tails. Bioluminescent worms the size of pythons poke out of crevices in the cavern walls. I spot human-faced octopuses and white salamanders.

The heads of long-necked beetles protrude from spun-glass cocoons. All of the creatures focus their attention on the altar.

A somewhat smaller version of the eyeball tree perches vertically there, the sawed-off trunk gripped by what looks like a stone Christmas tree stand. The tree gazes at us with one yellow, melancholic-looking eye, while all the others remain closed. The bony hands at the ends of the branches spread their fingers wide. On the stage, four pony-sized rabbits stare at the tree, their wings tucked in at their sides.

Ernie climbs a few steep stairs onto the raised platform. "Take a seat, everyone," he says, his voice slurring somewhat. "Wherever you want. Cool. Perfect."

Nichelle leads us to the pew closest to Ernie. Evangeline and Cassian and Topher join us.

Ernie steps to the edge of the altar and looks down at us. He says, "As you already know, during my childhood and early teenage years, I spent a good chunk of my summers at this park. The Goblin Chapel show was always put on at the end of the day, because this event takes place at the end of Binkler's story." Ernie walks backward and positions himself near the large rabbits. "One of the goblin elders stood about here. He wasn't a statue or an animatronic. He was played by a staff member in green, wrinkly makeup. After firing up the crowd, he introduced the huntress. Corinna, could you come up here and help us with the demonstration?"

I look at Nichelle and she shrugs, grinning.

Once I ascend the stairs, Ernie points to a spot beside him. He says, "The huntress stood about there. Perfect. Thanks for humoring me, Corinna." He licks his chapped lips. "The elder then gave a short speech about the battle and all the lives that were lost. Doctor Owl was banished, and his hybrid creatures were socialized and released into the forest. As for the Wolf King, he was knocked into his clockwork tower and crushed by the gears. I won't bore you with every minute detail of the speech. Afterward, the elder presented the huntress with sacred objects, honoring her for turning the tide of the war." Ernie picks up a couple of items from off a rabbit's back. He hands me a jewel-encrusted, foam ax and he places the woven reed crown on my head, decorated with acorns and pine cones and flowers. "Thank you, huntress, for your bravery and your sacrifices."

The Dredgers applaud and whistle.

Ernie pulls what looks like a TV remote out of his pocket and continues, "It was known that only a true hero could dispel the magic in the Wolf King's tree. So the huntress raised the sacred ax and chopped the tree. Go ahead, Corinna. After you strike the tree, take two steps back and stay there."

"Okay." I hit the eyeball tree with the foam ax and take two steps back.

I look over at Ernie who's busy pressing buttons on the remote.

After a few seconds, the eyeball tree shudders and jolts to life. Dozens of yolk-colored eyes open wide. The mouths curl their tattered lips to form gaping o's. Above, the tree's pale fingers bend in bizarre directions, and fog cascades onto the tree from above.

Suddenly, the tree lets out a multitude of preternatural howls. Gossamer phantoms erupt from the mouths, projected on the fog, soaring upward toward the stalactites. As the spirits continue to surge, the tree's eyes and mouths seal tight. The withered hands retract into the dark branches. Finally, the final phantom ascends, and the howling stops, and the tree beams with a thousand miniscule lights embedded in the trunk and branches.

For a moment, nothing else happens.

And then the pink-eyed rabbits spread their lustrous, golden wings. They thump their back feet against the altar floor in a steady beat. The cavern wall at the back of the altar breaks apart in slow motion, and a dozen or so goblins in sunshine-yellow gowns proceed onto the stage from the hole in the wall. The goblins swing their axes and shovels and hammers to the rhythm of the rabbits. They sing together in harmony, facing the pews, in some made-up goblin language. Most of their mouths move in-synch with their high-pitched voices, but some of the goblins seem to be malfunctioning. Throughout the cavern, the rodents and octopuses and all the other creatures sway to the music.

As the choir reaches a crescendo, the eyeball tree shines brighter and then the room becomes pitch black.

In this darkness, Ernie says, "And so all the lost souls trapped in the tree were free, and the Wolf King's reign over the living and the dead was finally at an end. That's where the show ended."

When the lights turn back on, the Dredgers applaud.

"Thank you all for indulging me," Ernie says, wiping sweat off his forehead with his sleeve. "I know the show's silly, but on an energy level, hopefully we've benefited from its message of freedom and celebration. Okay, that's it." He waves everyone away.

I head for the stairs and Ernie says, "Corinna, perhaps now's a good time for that conversation I mentioned earlier?"

I'm not in the mood for a one-on-one with Ernie, but at the same time, I'm curious to find out what he wants to tell me about Nichelle. I need to hear this.

I search the audience for Nichelle, and she's standing right next to the stage. "I'll be out in a minute," I say.

"I'll be at my tuffet," Nichelle says. "I'm nearing the end of my energy reserves."

As Nichelle and the other Dredgers pile out the Chapel, Ernie stretches his arms above his head and then sits on the floor next to one of the rabbits. He says, "Why don't you take a load off? We could be here a while."

I sit down on the altar and drop the foam ax.

Once everyone has left the chapel, Ernie says, "How to begin? I suppose I should start by saying that I'm somewhat of a sham, Corinna." He keeps his eyes turned down as he slowly turns the remote over and over in his hands. He says, "Every day, I wax poetic about authentic merriment, and yet true happiness doesn't come easy for me. As I mentioned the first night we met, I found no joy in my oceanfront property or my supercar or my girlfriend whose first name I can't even remember anymore. I've spent countless hours searching for who I am, and it's arduous, frustrating work. The labyrinth of my heart is particularly complex." He wipes the sweat off his face again with his sleeve. "Through my energy work, I managed to dredge up an early memory of me wandering around my yard, collecting roly-polies and pincher bugs in a little ceramic jar. When I captured an adequate amount, I brought the jar into my closet, and I sat across from an enormous nutcracker my grandpa gave me one Christmas. I fed the bugs into the nutcracker's mouth, and I crushed them, one by one. I don't know why I did that, but I remember how utterly satisfying it felt every time I heard a little crunch." He strokes the side of his remote with his thumb. "I've attempted to replicate that feeling by crushing insects, but that didn't work. I've tried rats and racoons and other vermin. It's an interesting experience taking the lives of animals, but I wouldn't say the activity brings me much joy."

What the hell. Is he serious? He looks up from the remove, right at me, and what I see in his eyes causes my chest to tighten up.

With a burst of adrenaline, I jump up and head down the stairs. I race down the center aisle between the pews. When I near the wooden entry doors, I can hear the lock clank. Nevertheless, I slam my hands against the door and tendrils of pain spread throughout my left hand. I think I just fucked up one of my fingers. Ignoring the pain, I press on the door as hard as I can.

Turning back around, I see Ernie standing at the edge of the altar with the remote in his hand.

I yell for help. I scream.

"You're wasting your breath," Ernie says. "This place is soundproof."

I keep trying the door. I keep yelling. I glance over at Ernie and he's still standing at the edge of the stage.

He says, "Calm down, Corinna. Relax your breathing. All I want is for you to listen to me. Once I'm finished, I'll let you go."

"I'm listening," I say, and while he speaks, I scan the cavern and scrutinize the walls and pews and floor for anything helpful.

"Thank you," Ernie says. "As I was saying, taking the lives of rats and racoons hasn't brought me much joy. You're probably thinking, 'didn't Ernie say he wanted to speak with me about Nichelle?' Well, I thought tempting you with information about your girlfriend would pique your interest and you would be more likely to stick around and listen to me." He starts pacing along the edge of the platform and says, "Anyway, after I started with the animals, I toyed with the idea of committing violence against another human being."

I can't find any alternative exits or weapons or anything at all. Why the fuck did I stop bringing my purse around with me in the park? Now I don't have my phone. I don't have my pepper spray.

Ernie's face glistens with sweat as he continues to pace, tossing the remote in the air and catching it again and again. He says, "Initially, the concept of vigilante justice appealed to me, and so I tracked down a horror of a man and hit him with my car."

My heart pounds even faster.

Ernie says, "At that time, I wasn't positive if I wanted to take a human life, so I let him off easy. I only broke a few bones. The vigilante experiment was enjoyable enough, and yet I knew there were greater exultations left for me to experience. During my meditations, I realized that the problem with George is that his energy reflects mine in too many ways. When I hit him with my car, nothing explosive occurred on a spiritual level. There were no sparks. Harming him was like pouring water into water. It was mundane. So I knew I needed a different kind of victim."

I know I should keep searching for a way out of here, but I can't help myself. I need to know. I say, "That's when you pushed Eff into the quarry?"

"What?" Ernie says, and he stops pacing. "I suppose I can understand how you would come to that conclusion, but Eff wasn't my type. There wasn't any real chemistry between us. As far as I know, Eff got drunk and fell into the pit."

I'd like to believe that Ernie's lying to me, but why would he keep the truth from me at this point? As far as I can tell, this is Ernie at his most honest. This is his feculent, festering inner self.

He continues, "I wasn't sure what kind of person I wanted as my first, so I spent some time wandering my labyrinth, trying to understand myself. In time, I unearthed a memory of my young teenage self, sitting in this chapel, staring at the huntress. She was beautiful, Corinna. I would sit in the front pew and imagine shrinking her down and carrying her in my pocket and squeezing her whenever I felt like it. I wanted to cut off her arms. I'd spent years attempting to push away memories like this, as you might imagine. I didn't want to be a monster, but this is the real me. Once I accepted that, a cosmic sense of relief washed over me. This is who I'm meant to be. As a child, I smashed insects. As a teenager, I wanted to crush the huntress's head with my nutcracker." He sits down at the edge of the stage, dangling his legs over the side. He grins at me, sweatier than ever. "When you showed up at the retreat, I knew you were the one I was waiting for. You look a little like the girl who played the huntress. You have similar eyes. And what I feel for you is otherworldly."

He runs his hand down his face, wiping off the sweat. He continues, "You're probably thinking, 'Isn't Selanthian a benevolent force? How could it bring me to this park to be sacrificed?' Well, that whole benign energy thing is merely a story I tell. The truth is, Selanthian is a goddess to some, and a demon to others. If she chooses you as one of her acolytes, she'll do whatever needs to be done so that you can unearth and fulfill your true desires. She'll orchestrate meet-cutes. She'll scratch your wife in her sleep to keep her away from you and your Hollywood lover. She'll bring you a girl who looks like the goblin huntress from your childhood. There are no limits to her power. He places his remote in his pocket and pulls out a hunting knife. He must have had the knife specially made, because the handle is bejeweled to look like the foam ax I was holding earlier. "Now that I've granted you access to my spiritual depths, we're both at our most vulnerable. This is the perfect moment." Ernie unfolds the blade of his knife. "I know I said I'd let you go after finishing this little speech of mine. I wanted you to calm down, but I promise that was my last lie to you. Everything else was more truth than I've ever given anyone."

He scoots forward, easing himself off the edge of the stage and dropping the few feet to the floor. He lands and staggers a bit. "Ouch," he says. "Fuck. Pardon my French."

I feel frozen in place, like one of the animatronic goblins on the stage. I need to do something. I need to move.

I take a deep breath. Think of this as just another performance. Think of this as a dream.

My fear is a tangled ball of cemetery worms wriggling in my torso, but I manage to take a few steps toward Ernie.

I clear my throat and continue forward. I say, "Look, I freaked out for a bit, and my more primal instincts took over. But I've calmed down and I'm accessing my deeper self again. I want you to know that when I first came to the retreat, I was lost and consumed by grief. I didn't know what to do. But through my energy work, I realized that I felt so disconnected from the world because I don't belong here anymore. I'm meant to be with my loved ones on the other side. I was too frightened to ferry my own soul across the veil, and I think that's why Selanthian brought me to you." I am now within a few feet of Ernie and still he hasn't moved. He's watching me, sweating, studying my face. He holds his knife down at his side. I continue, "I can tell that you're anxious about what you're about to do, but you don't need to be. This is what I want, despite my earlier freak-out. All that I ask is that you put that knife away and use your bare hands. This is a sacred moment between us, and I want to feel the touch of your skin as I cross the veil."

Ernie stares down at his knife with a confused look on his face, and this is when I rush forward. I tell myself that he's the one who pushed Eff into the quarry. I uncage my rage, and I shove the sadistic fuck with all my strength, pain flaring in my left hand. He stumbles backward. His head slams into the rocky-looking wall holding up the front of the stage. In a moment, he's lying on his back, still gripping his knife.

I approach him, and when he starts moaning, I stomp on his face with my boot. He yells and turns away from me, curling into a fetal position. With my hand shaking, I manage to grab the remote from his pocket.

Now I'm racing toward the exit, pressing random buttons on the remote. I can hear the eyeball tree awakening again, letting out more unearthly howls. While I'm running, I accidentally hit my foot against one of the pews, but I manage to keep my balance.

Behind me, Ernie says, "There's no defying Selanthian's will. There's no escape."

I glance back at him, and he's standing again, his nose bent to the side, his face a bloody mess. He's heading toward me.

I must have pressed the correct button at some point, because the door no longer repels my efforts to free myself. In a moment, I'm outside, and techno music blares all around me. One of the park's speakers must be malfunctioning, because along with the music, I can hear a crackling buzzing sound. I run as fast as I can away from the Chapel, and I feel as if I'm floating. What now? I should have stomped Ernie's face a few more times when I had the chance. Where should I go? Were the other Dredgers in on all this? Did they set me up as a sacrificial lamb for their leader? Should I yell for help or would that only make things worse? I look over my shoulder and Ernie's a few yards behind me, limping a bit but moving quickly.

After making my decision, I veer to the right and pass the lemonade stand shaped like a teapot. I pass the colossal human-faced octopus with swings hanging from his sprawled-out tentacles. There must have been some bezoar in that cookie I ate, because all of this feels a bit like a dream. Am I actually awake? Could something like this actually happen? The techno music fades as I head deeper into this quieter section of the park. I imagine Ernie catching up to me and plunging his knife into my chest from behind. I imagine him reaching around and slicing the blade across my throat. Thankfully, none of that happens.

As I hoped, I find Nichelle sitting on a small grassy mound, meditating with her open notebook on her lap and a pen in her hand. A massive spider with rabbit ears dangles by a metallic cable, dropping lower and lower toward her head. The outer wall of the park looms behind her. A light attached to the rampart shines down on the whole scene.

Beside the tuffet, I say, "Nichelle."

She opens her eyes.

I turn my attention to Ernie, and he's approaching us casually, his hands in his pockets, his face still a bloody mess.

"He tried to kill me," I say. "He locked me in the chapel. He . . . he has a knife. He's the one who's been killing all the animals."

"What?" Nichelle says. She stands, looking more than a little bewildered.

"She's the one who attacked me," Ernie says, motioning to his face. "She's not yet accustomed to potent Selanthian energies, and the power overwhelmed her senses."

"He tried to kill me," I say. "Seriously, Nichelle. He's a fucking killer."

Nichelle studies my face.

"She's in crisis," Ernie says, and he comes closer.

"Alright, that's far enough," Nichelle says. "Stay away from her."

Ernie sighs and pulls his knife out of his pocket. He says, "You know what, Nichelle? Fuck you. I didn't want to bring you into this, but if you're going to side with your girlfriend over me, I'll just have to extinguish your light as well."

He limps toward us, unfolding his hunting knife. His left eye's sealed shut, and snot oozes over his lips.

Nichelle walks closer to Ernie and says, "Let's talk about this. Let's—"

And Ernie swings his knife wildly at her face.

I take this opportunity to kick him in the balls. I miss and manage to kick his upper thigh instead. He yelps with pain, and Nichelle stabs her pen into the side of Ernie's neck. His eyes widen. He opens his mouth and lets out a bizarre gurgling sound. A bead of sweat falls off the tip of his nose.

When he raises his knife again, I shove him hard, like I did in the Chapel, and he falls. The back of his head slams against the pavement. After that, he doesn't move at all.

I grab his knife and return to Nichelle.

"Your forehead," I say.

Blood cascades down her face from the wound Ernie gave her. She's staring down at him, looking more heartbroken than anything else.

"You're bleeding," I say.

Nichelle presses one of her palms against her forehead. She says, "Are you alright?"

"Not really," I say. "But I'm not dead, so that's a plus."

I tap Ernie's leg with my boot and I half-expect him to lurch back into life like some horror movie villain. He doesn't.

"What the fuck?" Topher says, stepping into the light. He's wearing a goblin mask and moth wings.

"Call an ambulance," I say.

"Okay," Topher says. "But what happened, man?"

"Call an ambulance," Nichelle says.

Topher nods and rushes away.

There's nothing I'd love more than to get as far away from Ernie as possible, but I need to make sure he doesn't regain consciousness. So Nichelle and I sit on the tuffet and I keep the hunting knife on my lap just in case.

"I didn't know he was like that," Nichelle says, holding her hand to her forehead.

"I know," I say.

I probably shouldn't admit this, but as we wait for the ambulance or the police or whoever might be coming, I think about how much I'll miss this place. Aside from the homicidal demon-summoner, I'll miss the people. I'll miss Topher's fucked-up stories and Cecil's salutes and Evangeline's arguments with Cassian. I'll miss the late-night chats with Nichelle in our room where we talked about nothing. Soon,

I'm going to be plunged back into Seraphina's reality where I'll have to feel all her pain. But I need to go back. Eff means the world and a bean to me, and I want to see her again, even if I'm only at her bedside to watch her die. She would do that for me.

Nichelle sniffles beside me, and I put my arm around her. I don't believe in fate or destiny or whatever, but I can feel myself at a crossroads here. I could choose the road where I push Nichelle away, the way I've pushed everyone away since I lost dad and Aunt Gloria and my mother. Or I could choose the road where I trust my gut and let Nichelle in. I could tell her my real name. If Eff were here, she would squeeze my hand, and with all the earnestness in the world, she would tell me to follow my heart. Eff is ridiculous.

I don't know what the hell I'm supposed to do.

Nevertheless, I make my decision, and as the pink brilliance of sunrise spills over the horizon and the Revelries come to an end, I ask Nichelle if I can tell her another story.

ABOUT THE AUTHOR

Jeremy C. Shipp is the Bram Stoker and Shirley Jackson Award-nominated author of *The Atrocities*, *Bedfellow*, and *Cursed*. Their shorter tales have appeared in over 60 publications, including *Cemetery Dance*, *Dark Moon Digest* and *Apex Magazine*. Jeremy lives in Southern California in a moderately haunted Farmhouse.

Their twitter handle is @JeremyCShipp.

DID YOU ENJOY THIS BOOK?

If so, word-of-mouth recommendations and online reviews are critical to the success of any book, so we hope you'll tell your friends about it and consider leaving a review at your favorite bookseller's or library's website.

Visit us at www.meerkatpress.com for our full catalog.

Meerkat Press
Asheville